*For T.K. and Babs. C.W.*

First published in the UK in 2019 by Nosy Crow Ltd
The Crow's Nest, 14 Baden Place, Crosby Row,
London SE1 1YW, UK

Nosy Crow and associated logos are trademarks and/or registered
trademarks of Nosy Crow Ltd

Text © Catherine Wilkins, 2019
Cover illustration © Joel Holland, 2019

The right of Catherine Wilkins to be identified as the author of this work
has been asserted by her in accordance with the Copyright, Designs
and Patents Act 1988.

Printed and bound in Great Britain by Clays Ltd, Elcograf S.p.A.
Typeset by Tiger Media

Papers used by Nosy Crow are made from wood grown in
sustainable forests.

ISBN: 978 1 78800 536 4

www.nosycrow.com

# THE WEIRD FRIENDS FAN CLUB

CATHERINE WILKINS

# CHAPTER ONE

**Saturday 16ᵗʰ February**

*ERIN*

When she was my age, Charlotte Brontë had already written her first poem and was about to leave school to teach her younger sisters at home.

I think I'd be terrible at teaching Kiera, she never listens. I mean, we get on fine – she's only two years younger than me. But if Mum ever asks me to help her with her homework, we end up fighting.

Mum's had it in her head that I'm "the clever one" ever since Mrs Wilson first mentioned that I might go up to the top set in English. We're due to get a letter after the English departments' faculty meeting or whatever. I really don't want to go up.

And Kiera isn't remotely stupid anyway. She just doesn't care about homework.

I hope Kiera doesn't read this diary.

GET LOST KIERA!!!! (If you are.)

But seriously, there's nothing you would find interesting here. You're always saying I'm boring anyway, and this is literally a diary that Mrs Wilson MADE me keep, to help with my writing, so POOP OFF!!!!!! (Yeah, I went there.)

God, this is why I don't keep diaries! There is no privacy in this house. We're all on top of each other, even though there's only the three of us.

And, I say house, it's a flat really. A tiny, tiny flat that we've lived in since the divorce.

Kiera and I share a room (with bunk beds – retro AND space-saving). SHE is on the top because I didn't say "bagsy" quick enough and apparently Mum preferred the law of the playground to listening to "one more *ruddy* argument".

If I was trying to sell you my flat, I would tell you it was a cosy, one-and-a-half-bedroom apartment with an intimate kitchen-come-lounge and a bijou bathroom.

But I live here, so I can say the living room has a

cooker, sink and fridge in it, and the bathroom – and this is true, we measured it – is *smaller* than my best friend Nic's *actual bath*.

Now, to be fair, my best friend Nic does have quite a big bath in her family bathroom. Like slightly bigger than average. But *still*.

And my bathroom still *has* a bath in it. A tiny, tiny short, thin bath you can sort of sit in, to which we have added a Poundland showerhead attachment for a crouched, one-handed shower.

The sink is roughly the size of my hand, so you can squeeze past it to get to the toilet. The toilet is normal-sized. Whoever built this didn't care how we washed, but they wanted to make sure we could poo in relative comfort, which is something.

Because the sink is so tiny, if you turn on the tap too fast water goes everywhere. There's a knack to it that visitors often don't possess. And if more than one person wants to brush their teeth at the same time … well, it's basically like a Cirque du Soleil performance.

I don't hate my flat or anything. I actually kind of like it. It's ours. And we get along. For the most part. We're kind of all in it together. Not that it was ever us vs. my dad. Not exactly. He just has this weirdly competitive streak. Anyway.

I was supposed to write about why I like Charlotte Brontë. But instead I got distracted, and now Mum's calling me and – OH NO!!!! The letter came. *I'm going up a set in English.*

### GRACE

When she was my age, Charlotte Brontë had written one poem and was about to leave school (at fourteen!!) to teach her sisters.

I'd be brilliant at that. (Not leaving school at fourteen – I love school.) I mean the teaching. I'm an excellent communicator. I don't actually *have* any sisters, or any brothers, but in theory I'm pretty sure I'd nail it. And I've written *loads* of poems.

Here's one, just off the cuff:

*I'm Grace the writer,*
*My words can kill.*
*If you haven't heard of me yet,*
*Then you soon will.*

And that's just freestyle. I can do even better

ones than that.

I'm not saying I'm better than Charlotte Brontë. Not *yet* anyway. Ha ha. I am genuinely kidding. I love Charlotte Brontë.

I do a lot of *joke-boasting* in my friendship group. Everyone gets it. You'll get it when you get to know me, diary, but I've been told I can come across as up-myself at first. (But you know, only by *losers* who are jealous of my greatness.) Ha. Love and support to any enemies. #lovetomyenemies

This is the first writing exercise that Mrs Wilson has set. I mean it's not even really homework, it's just for me.

Basically, Mrs Wilson (my awesome English teacher) has spotted that I have the makings of a very talented writer and so she said I should start keeping a diary.

At first, I thought it was to document my early years as a writer (presumably as material for the museum that will one day be built about me). But it turns out she meant that it's good practice for writing. And for the short story competition I am going to enter (and win!).

The prize is amazing: you get to go and visit the

Brontë Parsonage Museum in Yorkshire and see the house that the Brontës lived in! *And* do a week's writing course and some nature walks on the moors!

I think Mrs Wilson is probably very impressed with how mature and sophisticated my tastes are. I don't think that many people my age have read *Jane Eyre*, it's not on our syllabus until G.C.S.E.

So anyway, as per Mrs Wilson's suggestion, to "get me going" here are some of the reasons why I love and identify with Charlotte Brontë:

1. She's an amazing writer who really conjures up a scene and makes you feel as if it happened to you.

2. She worked really hard and was very clever.

3. She spoke French and spent time in France, and I'm really good at French and *J'adore la France!*

4. I think I have a similar inquisitive mind and thirst for knowledge to Charlotte Brontë, because in her book, *Jane Eyre*, the young Jane Eyre preferred the more grown-up *Gulliver's Travels* to babyish fairy tales.

5. Her mum died of cancer when she was five, and my mum died when I was a baby, in a skiing accident.

That's enough listing for now.

# CHAPTER TWO

**Monday 18<sup>th</sup> February**

*ERIN*

Mum has some nerve calling me silly. Just because I don't want to go up to the top set in English.

"Wanting to sit next to your stupid best friend Nicole is not a good enough reason!" she screamed at me this morning. "Who knows if you'll even *be* best friends in two months? This is not how you make life decisions."

Like she can lecture me about life decisions.

Also, it's not a decision. Well, it's not MY decision. It's the school's decision. I have no say in it.

I'm annoyed Mum called Nicole stupid, too. She probably just has bathroom envy.

Actually, I'm pretty sure Mum doesn't like Nicole's mum because Nicole's mum only works part time, and once picked Nic up in her tennis outfit, and after they'd gone Mum kept remarking sarcastically how nice that must be.

So she also has tennis envy.

But it seems unfair to dislike someone just because they get to play tennis and you don't.

## *GRACE*

I'm so gutted for my friend Chloe. Just found out she's moving down two sets in English. So unfair. Our little group won't be the same without her. First day back after half-term and this happens.

She group-messaged us this morning, while I was brushing my teeth. (I'm writing this as Daddy's car drives me to school.) I was having *feelings* about it, so I thought I'd write them down. Because that's what writers do, and *I* am a *writer*.

Apparently, she'd had several warnings that her grades just weren't good enough to be in the top set. I wonder why her parents didn't just get her a tutor at the first sign of trouble? That's what Daddy would have done. Not that he'd ever need to with me.

I think Chloe is feeling quite down because we normally always sit together and she'll miss us (and, let's face it, all the gossip). No one wants to be left out. Even if we make an effort, there'll still be stuff she'll miss.

And, ALSO, she doesn't want to sit with the *numpties* in that group. She belongs with us. The whole thing is just really cruel.

I wonder if I should have a word with Mrs Wilson? Explain how we're a group, and we belong together?

I mean, I'm not saying I have *that* much clout, but maybe they haven't thought about it from Chloe's point of view? And maybe if she promises to work extra hard? And Mrs Wilson loves me, I'm top of the class.

And if Mrs Wilson says no, maybe we could still have a goodbye party or something? Or like, buy her a cupcake at lunch … if they have cupcakes today.

### ERIN

"All right, swot? Five days to go!" said Nic, instead of "hello", when we were waiting for registration. (Nic sometimes calls me swot as an affectionate nickname, and I'm *totally fine* with that.)

She was talking about the number of days till The Gig. (We're seeing one of her favourite indie bands, *The Crumples*, on Friday.)

I'm really lucky to be going, because Nic's parents have paid for my ticket too. And they're driving us and everything.

"Monobrow!" Theo Remis suddenly shouted across the form room at me. A few people sniggered. I looked away and pretended I hadn't heard.

Nic caught my eye. I thought she might say something comforting, like, "he's an idiot" and "there's nothing wrong with your eyebrows but instead she grinned and went, "Don't worry, I like your monobrow." Which didn't really help.

I sat there for a moment, feeling sorry for myself, and then I watched Grace Abella across the room, over-reacting to a fly. She was squealing and running about for maximum drama and shouting that it was a wasp. *Eurgh*. That girl is *extra*.

Her friends indulged her lunacy, and I caught Nic's eye again and we both laughed, shaking our heads. And then I felt a tiny bit better.

I wish Theo would stop calling me "monobrow"

though. Why are boys so horrible? Well, probably not all boys, just most of the ones I come into contact with at school.

I know there must be nice boys here too. Like … how Pete Hannan and Si Adoki sometimes high five each other in the corridor in way that looks quite friendly and non-threatening.

And Nick Brooker seems quite nice and civilised, and once maybe smiled at me in music – or he may have been wincing at the music being played, it's hard to say for sure. (I did a wincey smile back to cover all bases, so it's possible he thinks I'm weird now anyway.)

I don't fancy anyone. But if I *was* going to fancy someone, it would probably be one of those three boys, who have never shoved me or called me names. It's important to have standards. Haha. *Sheesh*.

One of the many reasons that I love Charlotte Brontë is that she gets it. She knows (knows?) *knew* what people are like.

What I mean is: sometimes I feel down and alone, and like I don't have very much in common with anybody else. And it's a sad, scary feeling, and it makes me feel a bit sick. Like I'm invisible, or that I might just float away.

And then I read *Jane Eyre*, with all her trials and tribulations, and how she learnt to depend on and trust herself, and I know I'm not alone, and other people feel the things I do, and it's like a tether, keeping me connected to the world, so I don't float off. And then I feel better again.

Like, I love how *spirited* ten-year-old Jane Eyre is – and funny! My favourite bit in the book is when this really horrible, religious (and hypocritical) headmaster (Mr Brocklehurst) comes to meet her, to see if she can come to his school. (He's been told all these lies about her because her cousins and aunt are horrible too.)

So he wrongly suspects her of being bad, and starts quizzing her about burning forever in a fiery pit in hell. And he asks her what she must do to avoid it, and she says, "I must keep in good health, and not die." I LOVE that!

And I also like the bit where she stands up for herself to her horrible cousins and shouts: "They are not fit to associate with me!"

I guess I like reading about characters that have the odds stacked against them, but still learn to stick up for themselves to their bullies. Maybe it gives me hope.

And if Jane Eyre can survive all that, I can survive school.

Oh look, I accidentally actually did the assignment. I'm not sure "reading *Jane Eyre* stops me feeling like a lost helium balloon" is exactly what Mrs Wilson intended.

I like and identify with Charlotte Brontë in other ways, too...

There's the whole Irish thing. What I mean is we're Irish. Well, we're a bit Irish.

Charlotte Brontë's dad came from Ireland and his name was originally Brunty, but he changed it to Brontë in the UK.

My dad's dad came from Ireland. We used to visit there a bit when I was younger. Then the relative who liked us died, so we don't go there very much any more.

Some of my Irish family don't really like English people. Which is historically understandable. But we're *technically* Irish.

At least Theo isn't in the top set for English. Just all the snooty people in my year, whose parents are doctors and bankers and whatever.

I'm not *loving* keeping this diary so far. It just feels like a list of bad things that are happening to me. Maybe as a writer, I'm supposed to put a more positive spin on things...?

I'm really not sure I'm a diary person. But if Mrs Wilson says it will help my writing, I will try for a bit longer. Especially as I want to enter that competition. I would LOVE to visit the Brontë Parsonage Museum. And I'd never be able to afford it otherwise.

### GRACE

What a day! First a wasp attacks me and then I can't convince Mrs Wilson to let Chloe stay in our English set.

I can't believe Mrs Wilson didn't listen to me. I mean, I *can*. But I still think she was a *bit* dismissive.

I certainly didn't interrupt her lunch with "childish nonsense" like Mr Porter said I did. That man is just rude. I am so glad I'm not in his group for P.E. And why was he even eavesdropping on our private conversation in the first place?

I came and politely found Mrs Wilson at an

appropriate time. It's hardly *my* fault we don't have English on Mondays; I didn't want to wait.

Poor Chloe.

It was kind of nice in the form room after lunch, before registration at least.

As a sort of joke, I started singing, "I will remember you, will you remember me?"

I started off low-key but everyone liked it, so I got a bit louder and did more dramatic actions.

Then the rest of our group joined in and we spontaneously sort of almost serenaded her.

I happen to be a really good singer, so shoot me. (I refuse to hide my light under a bushel, just because the world isn't ready for my greatness.)

But we're all quite good singers, so as we got louder and louder, there were actually some surprisingly nice harmonies going on.

At the end we all laughed and group-hugged Chloe. I think it was probably quite moving.

The rest of the form must have enjoyed it, because they clapped, and so I bowed. And someone even decided to show off that they could do that whistle noise.

Everyone had *loved* it. Well, almost everyone. That

grumpy girl with the mousy dark hair, whose name I can never remember – Erica? – was frowning at me.

She quickly looked away when she realised that I'd noticed her. Then she and her friend Nicole exchanged this smirk and rolled their eyes, shaking their heads. ABOUT ME. And my singing. The *cheek*!

Oh, *sorreee* little emo kids that probably listen to "cool" bands I have never heard of. *Sorreee* for liking classic mainstream pop music that doesn't make people depressed. *Sorreee* for caring about my friend and sharing my talent with the world.

Not that I care what those smug losers think. Ha! #lovetomyenemies

### ERIN

Oh noooooo. I was about to go to sleep, but Nic just texted to remind me that *Grace* is in top set English. Of course she is. I should have known that. Miss attention-seeking-behaviour herself, and the meanest of the crew of basic Barbies in the whole school. FAN-TAS-TIC.

Nic is finding this way too funny. I mean, she has sympathy too, but she just seems to think I'll have a laugh watching them be pretentious. But it's only fun watching them be pretentious when *Nic is there too*. Otherwise I'm just a loner sneering at people.

It's hard enough trying to zone out Grace's exhibitionism in the form room. Now it's going to be ruining my favourite subject too.

She was *singing* in the form after lunch today, for no reason, at the top of her lungs. So *annoying*. Like, we get it, you're amazing at everything, Grace. Leave *some* crumbs of activity for the rest of us.

Aaaaaarrrrggggghhhhhh!

OK. I'm starting to worry that my diary (and my attitude?) is too negative. So I am going to attempt to redress the balance and focus on something good in my life every time I have to write about something bad.

So, I will say this…

Dinner was excellent.

Comparatively anyway.

Mum brought home (or stole, depending on your perspective) loads of the "leftover" sandwiches from the meeting room at her work today.

It must have been an important client because there were also four bits of cake, three pieces of quiche, two scones and one huge packet of crisps. So basically, we ate like some kind of carb-obsessed Hungry Caterpillar.

*Waaaay* better than last night's dinner, when we had to share a tin of spaghetti hoops between three. Or would have, but Mum said she wasn't hungry.

At first Mum was embarrassed she'd had to stoop to this to feed us. But now she's sort of made it into an art form. She takes a massive handbag to work, full of empty Tupperware.

And it's not *really* stealing, because it would just be thrown away, or eaten by the temps, and they (probably) don't have kids to feed.

Mum worked her way up to her current job. She's one of the main PAs to the head of HR at this huge engineering company. It's a really busy place, she often has to work long hours, and because it's international, sometimes there are meetings by satellite at crazy times.

Mum is the only person in her department who doesn't have a degree. (She left school at sixteen and has had loads of different jobs.) This makes her determined that Kiera and I get good educations, while simultaneously claiming that she's the only person "living in the real world".

Mum likes to have her cake and eat it. And bring it home for us.

# CHAPTER
# THREE

**Tuesday 19ᵗʰ February**

***GRACE***
OMG. *D.R.A.M.A!!!* So #awkward today!

Grumpy *emo-what's-her-face* has been moved up to *our* Top English Set!!!!

WHAT!!!!!!

She has *usurped* Chloe! She is a usurper! OF ALL THE PEOPLE!!!!

First we realised was this morning in double English when she randomly came over to *our* table, didn't even make eye contact with anyone, and just tried to slink into Chloe's seat!

I get that it's the only free chair – but *where are her manners*? Say hello! Don't just jump into someone's grave like that.

We were all so shocked, but Sylvie was the first to recover, and said: "*Um?* You *can't* sit with us."

And Grumpy Face was about to reply, but that's when Mrs Wilson breezed into the room, all happy about it, going, "Oh great! That's it, sit down, don't stand on ceremony. Girls, Grace, show her the ropes!"

AND THEN she starts singing this girl's praises! Like she's some kind of genius. And how it's very exciting she'll be in our group, and she got an extraordinarily high score on the last something or other.

And I said, "Well, she may have been top of *Third Set* but she won't be top of *this* class." Because I really thought Mrs Wilson was getting carried away, and needed to be brought back down to earth.

And Mrs Wilson said, "Actually, Grace, that's why Erin's moved up. Her mark was a fraction higher than yours in the last assessment."

I honestly felt like I'd been slapped in the face. *AS IF* she's better than me. At ANYTHING. We will soon see about *that*, thank you, Mrs Wilson.

And then Mrs Wilson said: "Grace, I especially hope *you* will make Erin feel welcome, because you're both such huge fans of Charlotte Brontë."

My blood ran COLD. This little upstart is *not* stealing my place on that writing course too!

Mrs Wilson then swanned off happily to start the lesson.

I smiled scathingly at Erin so that she knew I was absolutely *not* going to make her feel welcome, and she needed to BACK OFF now.

"Welcome to the group," I said sarcastically. "*Sorry? What was it…? Erica? Elmo?*" The rest of my friends spluttered with laughter.

We definitely made sure she didn't feel welcome.

Ha. That'll teach her.


### *ERIN*

Oh. My. God. English was everything I feared and *more*!

I can't believe that stupid #youcantsitwithus hashtag has actually just happened to me in real life. I sometimes hate the modern world. Everything is a meme hidden inside an in-joke, and I don't know what's ironic any more.

Charlotte Brontë didn't have to worry about this nonsense. She only had to worry about *proper* problems. Like, well, typhoid and stuff like that. (I hear it.)

Parents worry about their kids being bullied online. But I managed to get it the #oldskool way. In person. By a gang of stuck-up predators that hate me.

They literally spent five minutes at the start of the lesson trying to rename me as something they'd "be able to remember".

I still can't believe they think I'm an *Emo*. (At least Nic thinks this is funny and that we should *up* it and start wearing Goth makeup.)

And they were actually quite personal about my face. And now I'm really thinking about plucking my eyebrows.

And it's Dad's weekend soon. I don't really want to go.

*Eurgh*. Everything is rubbish.

Happy thoughts. Happy thoughts.

I really must find a way to be chill about everything. What is the secret of that?

Dinner = half a tin of Heinz tomato soup and a piece of toast, followed by an apple. Can't complain. (About that.)

Had to hide my diary from Kiera just now and she

looked at me funny. Pretty sure it's still secret.

I pretended to be looking at my phone while she tidied some of her clothes away. I ended up scrolling through photos of how Grace spent her half term.

It's so ridiculous it almost cheers me up. These clowns can't bully me. Look at them.

In one, Grace has uploaded a picture of herself at the hairdressers. (Like, *what*? Since when are we supposed to share pictures of the hairdressers?)

She's done that classic pose in the mirror, casually holding the phone with her fingers in a V shape; and tagged herself with #beauty #loveit #treatyourself #ootd #howistyle #livingmybestlife *Eurgh*. Why don't I just puke all over my phone?

Also why has she put #ootd? You can't even see her *outfit of the day*, she's sitting down!

Come off it, Grace. You're just a person. You're not all that. And your hair always looks the same. Get over yourself.

I continue scrolling down and see a picture of her and her gang all dressed up and pulling "attitude" poses outside Byron Burger. She's captioned it "Girl squad on point. #youcantsitwithus #lovemylife"

*So basic.* Stupid sheeple.

For a second, I feel a mad urge to comment, "I DIDN'T WANT TO SIT WITH YOU ANYWAY!" all over her posts.

But then I take a mental step back and chuckle to myself. This is so ridiculous. Me and Nic would *never* post *our* hair appointments. We laugh at people who do that. I am above this. I just have to not let it bother me.

Not bothered.

Don't need to pluck eyebrows. It's *their* problem.

Definitely.

# CHAPTER FOUR

**Wednesday 20th February**

*GRACE*

Our campaign against Erin initially continued successfully in English today. She actually gave us this amazing target in her random, *super-mad* eyebrows. But then: MORE DRAMA.

"Oh my god, what did you do to your face?" said Sylvie, when Erin sat down.

"Oh. Wow. I think *someone's* tried to use an eyebrow pencil for the first time. Don't worry, you'll get there," I added patronisingly. And everyone sniggered.

She went satisfyingly red, and then the lesson started.

But then, after the bell rang, Mrs Wilson called Erin and me to stay back. For a horrible moment I thought she might have overheard what we'd been saying, but she hadn't.

She wanted to unveil her great PLAN for us: Mrs Wilson wants to start an extra-curricular Creative Writing Club at our school!

And *we* are her guinea pigs. Her patient zeroes, if you will.

Mrs Wilson gave us all the information about the Brontë-inspired writing competition.

Every year the winner gets money, prestige and is interviewed on the radio by that terrible DJ.

All the kind of stuff that looks good on a school's books. (Apart from the radio interview – but maybe that does too?)

Mrs Wilson wants us to practise writing short stories, meet up, and discuss them.

"Mark each other's work?" I asked, intrigued and appalled.

"Give feedback," Mrs Wilson corrected me. "It's called constructive criticism in literary circles."

"But isn't it better to just get *expert* feedback, like from you?" I persisted. (I have to say the part about *dishing out* advice appealed; not so much the receiving.)

"Well, this is how you develop critical skills," said Mrs Wilson. "And you might react differently to a piece of writing than I do."

She also suggested we *work together* to "do a bit of research" and find other short story writing competitions to "cut our teeth" on.

It adds up to quite a lot of extra work, but she doesn't think this is a problem, as we're both so clever and "passionate about Charlotte Brontë" and it's not our G.C.S.E.'s yet or anything because we're only in Year Nine.

In short, Mrs Wilson seems to want me to help my *enemy* apply for the thing I want most in the world.

"And I'm going to set you a few little writing exercises of my own now and then," Mrs Wilson revealed. "Maybe you have to write a letter in the style of Shakespeare or Jane Austen or something like that. Does this sound of interest to you, girls? I think you might find it really fun."

"Upon my word!" I joked, because I couldn't think of anything else to say.

"Great!" Mrs Wilson took this for acquiescence.

"So I can count on you? Oh hooray! How exciting."

We both clearly loved Mrs Wilson enough to comply. "Sure!" we both said, without making eye contact with each other.

Mrs Wilson then breezed out of the classroom, leaving us awkwardly alone together.

Erin just stood there mutely, so of course it fell to me to do something. I'm used to being very organised with my solo projects, so I suggested we swap numbers and start googling writing competitions.

Then Erin rudely interrupted and said, "Look, I'm sure you don't want to be seen talking to me. Our parents all have each other's emails. Just get your mum to ask my mum for details or something? We don't even have to meet up."

*What's that about?* And she totally *started* any animosity between us anyway, by always giving me evils and rolling her eyes behind my back.

"I don't care if I'm seen talking to you," I said honestly. "*Babe*, I'm popular enough to recover from *anything*. Even *you*. Joking. Is that how shallow you think I am? You emos are so judgemental."

I'm pretty good at getting in the zingers. She just claimed to not be an emo and kept on trying to get out of it.

"Look, our parents can't help us with this project and my dad has no desire to talk to your mum, I assure you. He's very busy."

"My mum's very busy too. Look I just meant –" She trailed off.

"You were trying to get out of it?"

"Well. Yeah." (At least she admitted it.) "And you don't want to either," she accused me.

"Maybe not. But I'm not missing out on extra credit from Mrs Wilson just because you're a coward. Now give me your stupid number."

That told her.

We finally agreed to meet up quickly after our next English lesson and discuss what we'd found.

**ERIN**

Eyebrows are a *nightmare*. Why are there so many rules about eyebrows and how do I keep falling foul of them????!!!

First, I finally cave and pluck my eyebrows (even though I'm well aware you shouldn't have to change yourself for bullies, and I sort of hate myself for doing it, but I just wanted the taunting to stop. And

I totally plan to have principles later in life when it doesn't matter as much.)

So then they're all red and sore and Mum's all "Oh you should have come to me, you've really over done it, blah blah," which is all great and Captain Hindsight of her because she wasn't even here before. And then she tells me to fill in the gaps with a pencil or some eye shadow, except she had to leave super early this morning too, so I had to guess at how to do it.

I HATE Sylvie and Grace and the rest of them. They are so mean. I still can't *believe* I have to sit with them in English.

Why can't Mrs Wilson spot that Grace is just a stone-cold bully? Why is she trying to make me hang out with her? Would she tell an innocent, bad-eyebrowed lamb to hang out with a hungry, evil, bad-eyebrow-hating lion? (I am the lamb in this scenario.)

EMAIL
16.42
FROM: MRS WILSON
TO: CHARLOTTE BRONTË FAN CLUB

SUBJECT: YAY NEW SUPER WRITERS' GROUP AND FIRST ASSIGNMENT

Dear Grace and Erin,

So pleased you're as excited about this project as I am.

Just a little fun one to get you started:

Re-write the story of *The Three Bears*.

Best,

**Mrs Wilson**

*Second in Department for English*

### *GRACE*

What the hell is that supposed to mean?

# CHAPTER FIVE

**Thursday 21<sup>st</sup> February**

*ERIN*

EMAIL
07.48
FROM: ERIN BROWN
TO: CHARLOTTE BRONTË FAN CLUB
SUBJECT: RE: YAY NEW SUPER WRITERS' GROUP AND FIRST ASSIGNMENT

Dear Mrs Wilson,
Is this the kind of thing you mean? (Attached.)
Best,
Erin

### *The New Three Bears* by Erin

Goldilocks saw through the sham of the Bears' marriage: separate beds in separate rooms. One bed soft and one bed hard.

She wondered how long they had been keeping up appearances. She wondered how they had ever got together with such different tastes in everything from food to furniture.

Or had opposites attracted at first? Maybe Mummy Bear had once found it endearing that Daddy Bear liked salt in his porridge, while she preferred sugar. But now the grind of making *three* different porridges each morning – including one for the baby – was just an annoying time-drain.

Maybe Daddy Bear had once loved how soft Mummy Bear liked her chairs to be, but eventually grew frustrated he could never get up from them easily and insisted they buy only hard beds and chairs.

Maybe that's how it came to a head. A stand-off between which bed the couple would sleep in together. By then neither could face backing down because everything had become about winning.

They had to keep up appearances for Baby Bear.

They had to keep going through the motions until the market picked up and one of them could afford the deposit to move out.

Goldilocks didn't know how it started, or how it got this far, but she knew this: Baby Bear's chair had been broken before she got anywhere near it. And she wasn't going to take the blame lying down.

### *GRACE*

That little suck up. Handing it in *first*. My story is going to be WAY better than that…

Right…

…Ummm…

Once upon a time… No…

There once was a… No…

A long time ago… Aaarrrgghhh, no.

I've got it.

EMAIL

19.24

FROM: GRACE ABELLA

TO: CHARLOTTE BRONTË FAN CLUB

SUBJECT: RE: YAY NEW SUPER WRITERS' GROUP AND FIRST ASSIGNMENT

Dear Mrs Wilson,

Mine is now attached. I would have had it in sooner, but there was a netball match. I do lots of extra-curricular activities. Probably more than Erin. Anyway.

Best,

Grace

### *The Bears* by Grace

Everyone was prejudiced against Goldilocks. Just because she was blonde and beautiful, they thought she was stupid, but she wasn't. She was actually very clever. Probably one of the cleverest in all the land.

The others had dared her to break into the Bears' house because they thought she wouldn't be able to do it. They thought she'd be too scared. That's why they'd bet her one hundred pieces of gold.

But Goldilocks was brave. She wasn't scared of bears. She would win this dare just like she won everything. They underestimated her and that would be their downfall.

It would be the easiest gold she'd ever made. And they would learn not to mess with *The Locks* (a nickname she was trying out on herself to see if it would catch on).

Goldilocks staked out the Bears' place and wrote down their comings and goings in her cool little notebook with the purple butterflies on it. Once satisfied, she made her plan. She waited until she saw them slide the little key under the plant pot and the coast was clear.

Quaint that they would go for a walk, waiting for their porridge to cool down. Goldilocks shook her head and chuckled as she entered the property.

Her mission was to steal a bowl of porridge, search for the treasure – if indeed it existed, break a chair and get photographic evidence. But she decided to have a good look round first.

The living room looked normal. Mundane. Chairs, books. No obvious secret panels anywhere…

The rumours that the Bears kept treasure in their house were thought to have originated from Daddy Bear himself. They said he boasted sometimes. "I've still got my treasure," he'd say.

The kitchen seemed clean also. Table laid, cups and bowls. Hot porridge waiting to be eaten. There were two of everything, just like she expected. A Daddy one and a Baby one…

Goldilocks went upstairs. Baby Bear's room

looked much as she'd thought it would, as did the bathroom and Daddy Bear's room. But there was one last door at the end of the corridor…

Goldilocks could tell it was special. The carpet was thicker outside. Like no one walked here, like Baby Bear wasn't allowed to play here. This was clearly a room that must never be disturbed.

Cautiously, Goldilocks pushed the door and went in. Everything was white and pale blue. The room felt feminine. There was a beauty stand with a mirror, brush and single framed photograph. There was a smell of perfume so faint, Goldilocks wasn't sure if she'd imagined it.

This was *her* room, Goldilocks realised. Nothing had been touched or moved. Everything had been preserved just the way Mummy Bear had kept it.

Goldilocks took another step forward. She could now see that the photo frame contained a picture of a new-born Baby Bear. It was a cheesy, sentimental frame that said the words, "MY TREASURE".

EMAIL

19.41

FROM: MRS WILSON

TO: CHARLOTTE BRONTË FAN CLUB

SUBJECT: RE: RE: YAY NEW SUPER WRITERS' GROUP AND FIRST ASSIGNMENT

Well done girls!

You've both done this assignment much quicker than I expected! Since you're both so keen, shall we meet up tomorrow (Friday) lunchtime to discuss? I can chair the first meeting to show you how it's done, and then you can take it from there...?

I've only got a very tight window but I'm sure we can fit this in. Meet at the very start of lunch outside the Sixth Form stairs. I've arranged for you to use a corner of their common room. Don't be late!

Make sure you've read each other's stories and made a couple of notes by then. Nothing too detailed. It's just a bit of fun and good practice.

So pleased you're both so passionate!

Best,

**Mrs Wilson**

*Second in Department for English*

# CHAPTER SIX

**Friday 22nd February**

*ERIN*

OMG Grace. *Insecure much?* "Ooooh I'm so special, I do loads of extra-curricular stuff, Mrs Wilson. I do more than Erin. So I must be better. Please let me be bestest, Mrs Wilson."

Just goes to show, though. Here I am feeling jealous of Grace because I hate people who seem to sail through life so effortlessly. And it turns out she's not even enjoying it, because she's too worried about what everyone else is up to.

*Why* be annoyed about who handed it in first? Her story was (I hate to say it) quite impressive. She should relax and enjoy being good at stuff.

Grace and I arrived at the Sixth Form stairs while the lunch bell was still ringing. We're both *superfast*. *Super-keen*. We had to wait five minutes for Mrs Wilson to show up. No small talk, natch. Just painful silence. I hate painful silence.

"It's not too late," I joked eventually. "I could just get my mum to email your mum our notes, and we won't even have to communicate."

Grace scowled at me, spelled the word "D-a-d" like I was a tiny child learning to speak, and then went back to her phone.

Mrs Wilson bustled us inside, made a loud announcement to a couple of Sixth Formers that we're randomly allowed to be here, and then we all sat down on surprisingly comfy (if a bit worse for wear) soft chairs in the corner of the room. It must be nice being a Sixth Former.

Mrs Wilson "kicked us off" by telling us we're both great, then more or less invited Grace to insult me. At least, that's certainly how Grace seemed to interpret the sentence: "So Grace, what did you think of Erin's *Three Bears* story?"

"I thought it was derivative," said Grace snidely.

"Wait, *what*?" I blustered, not quite meaning to

react that way.

"Yeah," Grace smiled. "I thought it was really derivative."

"Well of course it was derivative!" I spluttered. "It was *the story of Goldilocks and The Three Bears!* It was *literally* derived from another thing. How could it have been anything but derivative?"

"OK. I think we're getting off track a little bit," said Mrs Wilson. "I think for now, let's stay away from big pronouncements like it was good or bad or *derivative*, and talk about how different bits made us *feel*." She looked between us to check we were both properly listening. "OK?"

We nodded.

"So Erin, what did you think of Grace's story?"

The annoying thing was, I actually liked Grace's story. I genuinely (if begrudgingly) thought it was quite moving towards the end, with a good twist, but I could hardly say that now that she'd slagged *mine* off.

"Um ...well," I replied awkwardly. "I thought it was a bit repetitive at the beginning."

"Which bit?" Grace seemed incensed.

"The beginning bit," I said. "It just keeps going on

about how brave and great Goldilocks is, and how much everyone will regret messing with her. Like, we get it already. You maybe could have done that in a more concise way."

Grace looked hurt and angry and Mrs Wilson put her hand up to Grace as if to stop whatever outburst she was about to make.

I quickly added, "I liked the ending, though."

"Ah, yes!" Mrs Wilson seized on this moment of positivity. "It *was* a very interesting ending, Grace."

Grace looked momentarily mollified and then haughty once more.

"I liked the twist," I said. They looked at me.

"You know," I continued, dutifully, "um, that 'The Treasure' has been Baby Bear all along? And people wrongfully have the impression that the Bears have some hidden gold. Was that…? Did I … *interpret* that correctly?"

"Yes." Grace nodded, seeming pleased.

"Very good," said Mrs Wilson.

(Though I honestly wasn't sure if she was talking about Grace's writing or my deducing skills. Or maybe the combination of both in action meaning her group was a success?)

"And I think," Mrs Wilson continued to Grace, "you've drawn on your own experiences with loss to conjure up such a moving picture of the house?"

"Yes," Grace nodded seriously.

*Own experiences with loss.* My brain suddenly reached the glaringly obvious conclusion as to why Grace had spelled out D-a-d for me, like I was a tiny child.

"Ohhh!" I blurted. "Your mum died!"

Mrs Wilson and Grace both stared at me.

"I'm sorry!" I sort of yelled. Then more quietly, "I'm so sorry. I didn't … and that's why you… I can't believe I didn't… I kept saying Mum. God. I'm *really* sorry."

There was a terrible pause, during which Grace stared at me. Then she raised a haughty eyebrow, with a touch of amusement on her lips, and said, "And I thought you were meant to be *clever*."

And then she did this sort of smirk, but like it was an invitation for me to smile too. Like she was letting me off the hook.

"Oh!" I laughed nervously. "I'm so sorry."

"It's fine." Grace put up a hand, magnanimously but also curtly. I felt like she was signalling that the

44

subject was now closed.

"So Grace, do you have any more constructive criticism about Erin's story?" asked Mrs Wilson. "Now that we're all ... getting the hang of it."

(How was me shouting "Your mum died!" getting the hang of it?)

"Um, well ... I guess I was starting to get intrigued by how the chair got broken at the end," said Grace. "But then it just finished. Was it meant to be a cliff-hanger?"

"Um, kind of," I said. "I sort of just ran out of time."

"Right," said Grace, sounding decidedly underwhelmed. "So what happens next?" she addressed Mrs Wilson. "Do you mark us now?"

"No, this is just for you. There are no marks," said Mrs Wilson.

"Yeah, but like, whose was best?" persisted Grace. "I mean, mine, obviously. It was longer and better written."

"No, we're not judging it like that. And even if we were, as you know, in my class, longest isn't necessarily the best. I award marks for style, content and being succinct as well."

"So Erin's was the best?" queried Grace.

"No. Look. We're practising our writing skills in a constructive and supportive setting," insisted Mrs Wilson.

"But how will that help us to get ahead?"

"By *honing your skills*." Mrs Wilson sounded the tiniest bit vexed. "So much of the syllabus now is about hitting targets and ticking boxes. And those things *are* important, but creativity doesn't always work like that. I think it's important to have a space where the learning and the journey is as much fun as the result. Oh gosh, is that the time. I have to go. Well done, both! To be continued!"

And then she bustled away again.

"Riiight," said Grace, but she didn't sound completely convinced.

"So, bye, I guess –"

"Are you really – "

Grace and I spoke over each other. "Sorry, what were you going to say?" I asked her.

"Are you *really* a Charlotte Brontë fan?" Her eyebrow was quizzically and yet haughtily raised again.

"Yes, she's my favourite author!" I gushed.

"What do you think was wrong with Bertha Mason?"

I couldn't hide my surprise. "Um, I think it's widely considered now to have been Huntington's disease, isn't it?"

"Have you read *Villette*?" Grace surveyed me coldly, eyebrow still up.

"Yes. Is this some kind of *test*?"

"Virginia Woolf said it was better than *Jane Eyre*."

"I know."

"Do you indeed. Do *you* like *Jane Eyre* best?"

"I—"

"All right, Elmo, don't worry." She stood up to go.

"Oh thanks, *your majesty*," I said sarcastically.

She shook her head at me and walked off, chuckling.

### GRACE

I wish Mrs Wilson would stop beating about the bush and just tell us who is best. It's exhausting trying to work it out for myself.

I don't even care if it's not me at this point. I CAN TAKE IT. *Don't treat me with kid gloves!* If it's not me – I CAN UP MY GAME! And then win

later. (And then drink the tears of my haters, haha.)
#lovetoanyenemies

It might sound weird to write this, but it's MY diary so it doesn't matter. And also, as a writer, it's important to examine your dark side too and be self-aware... I think Erin has brought up some feelings in me that I haven't felt for a long time. I think it might be jealousy.

I don't have any brothers or sisters, but I'd always assumed I'd be quite good at sharing. I mean, I'm *very* generous when it comes to food or money.

But maybe I want Mrs Wilson's praise just for myself. I don't want to share Mrs Wilson with Erin. Or the English top spot. Or the writing competition prize.

I wonder if this makes me a bad person...?

No. I'm wonderful.

I mean, look at my track record. I've done loads for charity: two fun runs, four bake sales, that fashion competition, the Guinness world record attempt at who could take the most selfies in one minute... The problem is *not* me.

It's far more likely that Erin is an awful witch with evil magical powers holding Mrs Wilson to ransom with some terrible spell.

### ERIN

"Oh my god, we're going to be telling our grandkids about this gig!" Nic assured me excitedly, as I watched her try on her fourth outfit. "Zip me up?"

Whenever we do something fun like this, Nic always wants me to come to her house so we can "get ready together", but I am always already ready as I have basically one outfit. My #ootd is the same every day. Well, every weekend day.

"Seeing as you're ready, can you just plug my hair straighteners in? I want to do my fringe again. And, actually, can you go downstairs and get some crisps and lemonade? Ta."

I know I'm lucky to be here (and to get free crisps and lemonade). And hang out and everything. But sometimes it seems like I have to do lots of stuff for Nicole. I don't mind, though. She *is* my best friend.

I guess *sometimes* I wish she wouldn't mock me for not knowing as much about music as her. And maybe I *should* have got around to listening to those songs she suggested on Spotify? I'm just not as into it as she is.

OMG, the gig was loud!!! I was so glad I brought earplugs (which I can never tell Nic about). It was one of those mid-sized venues that isn't so big you think you'll get lost but still big enough that there's no way you're going to the toilet on your own.

Nic's parents drove us all the way there and all the way back. (They had dinner in the restaurant next door while the gig was on because we're fourteen now. They used to come in with us.)

I *know* I'm so lucky. Soooo lucky. It was *so* kind of Nic's parents to pay and take us. And I know I'm definitely *supposed* to enjoy music, so I'm sure I will eventually.

I sometimes worry I'm being a teenager wrong. I'd much rather curl up at home and read *Jane Eyre* again than be crammed into a dark, sweaty fire hazard of a building.

And Nic always wants to go right to the front and try and dance, even though it's so squashy.

Look. I didn't *want* to be the teenager with the earplugs at the back. But I guess that's just who I am.

# CHAPTER SEVEN

**Saturday 23<sup>rd</sup> February**

*GRACE*
A poem by Grace Abella

*Always working, working hard,*
*I must because I'm clever.*
*Pretenders want to steal my crown,*
*But they will beat me never.*
*Always winning, winning best,*
*I do because I'm clever.*
*Pretenders wish they had my skills,*
*But I will win forever.*

#nailedit #livingmybestlifebabes

# Sunday 24th February

*ERIN*

Eurgh. Dad's weekend. At least we only ever stay one night.

It's always the same routine:

Mum drops us off at the café near his road on her way back to work *on a Saturday*; he lets us order food then ignores us and reads the paper. Then we go back to his flat, and he ignores Mum's instruction not to let us watch TV until we've finished our homework.

This time in the café, even Kiera realised Dad wasn't listening while she was rabbiting on about forming a Year Seven dance troupe with her friends. He just kept saying, "uh huh" and "mmm hmm" interchangeably.

Eventually she glanced at me and we exchanged this look of amused understanding, which made me feel impressed at how grown up and sophisticated my sister is at eleven, but also sad that she knows she's got a dad who doesn't listen to her. I feel like she deserves better. But Kiera just grinned at me and shrugged.

Kiera took full advantage of Dad's not-listening

skills when we got back to his flat and he gave her the TV control. She immediately put *Stranger Things* on Netflix and settled in to binge-watch. She's a bit obsessed with that show. While Mum worries that it's too scary, Kiera correctly identified that Dad would have no such objections.

Dad said he was working and replying to emails on his phone, but then it made a beep noise like he was playing a game so he put it on silent.

I did some homework on my computer and then started researching writing competitions. I used my tried and tested method of research and typed "writing competitions" into Google. There are loads! *Loads*. Just looking into them is like a job in itself.

It took me a little while, but I finally found one that might be suitable.

It's for young people (ages 12-18). It's free to enter and there's actually a money prize. It's 500 words and it has to be about ghosts…

I'd love to write something that Grace couldn't call derivative. As much as I still really don't like Grace, I did kind of enjoy being involved in a literary discussion…

Honestly, *literary discussion*. Who do I think I am?

We were talking about *The Three Bears*! We all took it so seriously. Is this why Nic and I usually mock people in "The Arts" for being pretentious?

———

When Kiera and I were getting ready for bed at Dad's, she handed me this flyer she'd found in the café and forgotten to tell me about. "Have you seen this?"

"Oh my god, there's a play about the Brontës! In our local… Damn, it's a tenner."

"It's only seven pounds for students, you can afford that."

"Maybe…" I pondered. "Do you want to come too?"

"Pass," said Kiera blithely. "Unless, like, no one else will go with you. Surely Nic will?"

Maybe Nic *would* love to come? I always do *all* the things *she* wants to do, like see bands and stuff. Maybe she'll be delighted I've finally got a suggestion of something great and interesting we can do together?

We nearly got through the Dad visit with no rows but, when Mum came to pick us up, the TV was on again. Dad clocked her gaze and said, "Oh, I've only just put that on."

But then – with sitcom timing – a message came up on the screen: "Would you like to continue watching *Stranger Things* on Netflix?"

So, Mum knew (a) he was lying and that the TV had been on ages and (b) Kiera had nearly finished watching all of *Stranger Things* against her wishes.

I hate it when my parents row. But at least it doesn't happen very often any more.

Anyway. Positive: Dad let us get takeaway fish and chips for dinner. Pretty happy about that.


### GRACE

My favourite part of the week is Sunday lunch because Daddy never misses it. He works very crazy hours the rest of the time, but Sunday lunch is *ours* and that's when we catch up. Plus, he always books somewhere amazing to eat.

This week he booked us into *La Saison Sol*, which is a wonderful French brasserie. Everything smelled divine when we arrived, and the waiter took our coats and led us to this lovely booth table, all laid out with gorgeous glasses and shiny cutlery.

Daddy and I started to talk about what we had each been up to all week. He was (of course) very

impressed that I am doing *another* extra-curricular thing.

"Well done, Abella!" He reached across the table and clapped me heartily on the shoulder.

(Daddy sometimes addresses me by our surname, like we're in the army or the all boys' school that he went to.)

Some people think Daddy can be a bit ... brisk or even rude. But I find him refreshingly frank and up-front.

"So who won this *Three Bears* competition?" Daddy took a sip from his aperitif.

"Oh, well, no one really. Apparently winning wasn't the point," I replied.

"Uh oh." Daddy rolled his eyes scornfully. "It's not one of those nanny-state, everyone's-a-winner, namby-pamby, hippy load of nonsense, is it?"

"No! Nothing like that. It's a *process*. Like training. Like you and karate."

"When I was learning karate, there were lots of fights and there was always a winner." Daddy put his napkin on his lap.

"I'm pretty sure I was the winner. I certainly should have been, anyway."

"That's my girl!" Daddy smiled appreciatively. "You don't get anywhere in this life without *killer instinct*. What do we say?"

"Second place is first loser," I recited dutifully.

"That's right." Daddy leaned back as the waiter brought over our entrées.

"Cheers, darling!" We clinked glasses and tucked in.

"This is delicious!" I declared.

"Mmm!" Daddy agreed with his mouth full and then swallowed. "I tell you what, Grace, if you ever learn to cook like this…" He paused.

"Yes, Daddy?"

"I'll be very disappointed." He grinned. "Because it will mean you're not spending enough time studying or bettering yourself. You don't need to learn to cook. Get rich like me and then pay people to do it for you."

And then Daddy told me all about *his* week. Daddy specialises in corporate and real estate law, so he spends most of his time finding loopholes to re-zone conservation sites for development. He is very good at it and loves his job.

## ERIN

EMAIL

19.41

FROM: ERIN BROWN

TO: CHARLOTTE BRONTË FAN CLUB

SUBJECT: RE: YAY NEW SUPER WRITERS' GROUP AND FIRST ASSIGNMENT

Dear Mrs Wilson and Grace,

I did a little bit of research over the weekend and think I might have found a short story competition that we could both enter as writing practice. It has to be 500 words and about ghosts (link below). I thought it looked OK. YMMV.

Best,

Erin

EMAIL

21.13

FROM: MRS WILSON

TO: CHARLOTTE BRONTË FAN CLUB

SUBJECT: RE: RE: YAY NEW SUPER WRITERS' GROUP AND FIRST ASSIGNMENT

Dear Erin,

What does YMMV mean? Not Roman Numerals?!

Please talk to me in English. I am an English teacher. And I also don't have time to Google slang. Thank you.

But well done, the competition looks good!

Let's meet at start of lunch on Monday (tomorrow) and have a quick discussion.

Best,

***Mrs Wilson***

*Second in Department for English*


EMAIL

21.34

FROM: ERIN BROWN

TO: CHARLOTTE BRONTË FAN CLUB

SUBJECT: RE: RE: YAY NEW SUPER WRITERS' GROUP AND FIRST ASSIGNMENT


Dear Mrs Wilson,

Sorry. YMMV means "your mileage may vary".

Best,

Erin

# CHAPTER EIGHT

**Monday 25ᵗʰ February**

*GRACE*

Hahaha, Erin got told off. This is already a great start to the week for me. I mean #lovetomyenemies sure. But also, hahaha.

Though I have to say, I was tickled picturing Mrs Wilson puzzling over YMMV. I guess it's understandable that Erin thought Mrs Wilson was cool enough to have known that. Though maybe she did, and she had to just *be a teacher* and tell us to write properly?

I am going to write a *brilliant* ghost story.

I love Mondays. I love catching up with all my friends and hearing what the people I didn't see at the weekend got up to.

Chloe got a new hamster because her mum wanted to cheer her up after she'd been moved down in English. (Just between you and me, diary, I think that's sort of the problem, right there. You'd never catch Daddy rewarding failure like that. Oh well. To each their own.)

#liveandletlivebabes


### ERIN

"What do you *mean* no way?" I was utterly baffled by Nic's response to my brilliant suggestion.

"I mean no way, obviously," said Nic. "I'm not a swot like you, I wouldn't enjoy a Jane Austen play at all."

"Charlotte Brontë," I corrected.

"Whatever. Boring."

"But … but … how do you *know* you wouldn't enjoy it? Unless you try it?" I attempted.

"Why would I want to go on what sounds like a *school trip* in my spare time?" asked Nic.

"Because it would be fun! And interesting. And *I* do loads of stuff *you* like, like music and stuff, why don't you try one thing *I* like?"

"But you like music too, don't you?" Nic was unmoved.

"Well, kind of, yeah," I lied. "But not as *much* as you."

"Oh sorreee." Nic was sarcastic. "Sorry my parents paid for you to come to a music gig you only *quite* liked. Tell you what, how about you pay for me to come to this stupid play, and maybe I will."

Ouch.

I couldn't *believe* Nic had said that. And, also, I could *never* afford to pay for both of us.

## GRACE

I was pleased to note I arrived *before* Erin for this lunchtime meeting. Only by thirty seconds or so, but start as you mean to go on. I think she was having an argument with her emo friend Nicole, but they were slightly out of earshot so I couldn't be sure. Ha. Trouble in paradise. Or at least trouble in the *Little Shop of Horrors*.

Haha, I'm so funny, must use that in English when we're next tormenting Erin. I'm in a *great* mood today.

Mrs Wilson is very happy with the ghost story

comp. But the deadline is ages away, so in the meantime she wants us to write a letter of complaint about a disgusting hotel room. In the style of Jane Austen.

"And this time," Mrs Wilson revealed, "I want you to take on board each other's feedback and work it into a re-write."

I did not like the sound of that one bit. *Pretending* to take on board Erin's terrible advice is one thing. But actually being forced to act on it? No, thank you.

"So, like, do a second draft?" asked Erin.

"Precisely," continued Mrs Wilson. "Write your letter, email it in. Make notes for each other, then meet up and share them *constructively*. I don't think you need me for that bit, now you've got the hang of it. Then both do a re-draft and email it in again."

"What if we don't agree with each other's criticism?" I asked.

"That's a good question," said Mrs Wilson. (I mean, obviously it was – I asked it.)

"Thank you," I couldn't help but reply. (Erin better not have rolled her eyes.)

"This exercise is about seeing if the changes make the overall work better or worse," explained Mrs

Wilson. "And good practice should you ever get into journalism, or any other kind of writing career where an editor gives you feedback."

"Journalism?" asked Erin then.

"Yes," said Mrs Wilson. "Right, I must dash." And she bustled off again.

### ERIN

I really don't get what Nic's problem is. First she won't do anything I like; then she's annoyed *I* have to do something I like.

So what if I have to miss the first part of lunch – for like five minutes. It's nothing! I still see her *all the time* – apart from English – and I only forgot to ring her sooner at the weekend because I was at Dad's.

And then Nic was like, "Fine, instead of your stupid play, I'll just join your stupid book club."

And I was like, "You can't just *join*, there's a process." But I promised I'd ask Mrs Wilson, even though I had no intention of asking because I knew full well that Nic only wanted to join so she could mess about. And then she would spoil everything.

Does that make me a terrible friend? It's not even like it's super fun. But it *is* super interesting. And like nothing else I've ever really been involved with. And the thought that I could be a journalist is AMAZING. *Me!*

I was so shocked by what Mrs Wilson had said that I forgot to dash off and find Nicole, and instead said out loud to Grace, "I wouldn't have thought *I* could be a journalist."

"Well, not with *that* attitude," Grace admonished me. She might have been joking; I couldn't tell.

"No, I mean, journalism's a blood bath," I explained. "There's no money in it any more. Print is dead, there's fewer and fewer jobs…" I trailed off.

"Erin, you're very defeatist." Grace seemed to be enjoying scolding me. "We can be anything we want to be, if we work hard enough."

Hmm. Maybe *she* can. With all her family connections.

"No, we can't," I said. "It's like that Chris Rock stand-up bit."

"Who?"

"Whoa! Do you not know who Chris Rock is?" I couldn't hide my astonishment.

"No, I'm kidding, of course I know who Chris Rock is," replied Grace.

I didn't push it, but she kind of looked like she didn't.

"Just remind me of the bit…?"

"You know? That bit where he says stop telling kids they can be anything they want to be? He goes, 'You can be anything you're *good at*, as long as they're hiring.'"

"Ha," Grace chuckled. "That's funny. And sad. Kind of sounds like our careers advisor actually."

I laughed. "Yeah! Oh man. Did you take that computer quiz of hers? Mine told me I should be a dog-walker. Which I would actually enjoy. But my mum would kill me."

"Oh god yeah. Daddy would go ballistic if I— Isn't that your friend?"

I looked up and Nicole was lurking by the door. When I looked up she tapped her watch theatrically.

"I'd better go." I started grabbing my bag. "I don't mind when we do this. And I'm happy to meet up anywhere, I don't mind." I waved over my shoulder as I dashed out.

**GRACE**

OK. I've Googled Chris Rock now. I really should

have heard of him. And I have seen him in films.

I started today on top of the world. One encounter with Erin and I feel like an *uncool teacher* who has to Google slang.

And every time I start to think she might be funny or nice, she does something horrible.

As I walked past her and Nicole on my way out of the common room, I heard her say, "But I don't even *like* Grace."

So fine. The feeling is mutual. Just you wait till English, Emo. In fact, why wait till English? Let's up this. You don't mind where we do the work? Then I'll pick somewhere. Somewhere an under-confident, insecure nobody like you will feel very uncomfortable...

That will teach you to lord it over me in English, while my good friend Chloe is reduced to surrounding herself with *Cricetinae* rodents for comfort.

# CHAPTER NINE

**Tuesday 26ᵗʰ February**

*ERIN*
EMAIL
20.52
FROM: ERIN BROWN
TO: CHARLOTTE BRONTË FAN CLUB
SUBJECT: JANE AUSTEN LETTER

Dear Mrs Wilson and Grace,
My letter is attached.
Best,
Erin

## JANE AUSTEN LETTER OF COMPLAINT — ERIN

Jane's House
Winchester
Hampshire
England

Twenty-seventh of January 1815

The Terrible Inn
Terrible Street
Really Bad Town
England

Dear Sir or Madam,

I had cause to stay at your establishment on my way to M—shire last week. It was a most grievous experience, and I am most vexed with you.

Our party arrived at the allotted hour, our horses taken care of and our luggage also. (This much I am obligated to credit you with. But this much alone!)

Your host then showed me to my quarters. Forsooth! A most terrible smell did fill my nostrils.

I intimated my displeasure at the stench and was greeted with a most supercilious retort of the sorts I shall not repeat here; rest assured the language was not at all acceptable to polite company.

When I intimated further that I absolutely could not stay in such a noxious room, I was informed that the previous occupant had been unwell. I daresay they had expired there, the stench was so potent!

I was then led to a much smaller room with barely space for a single bed, clearly a part of the servants' habitations. (At least the bouquet was no longer the pungent miasma of death.)

I did not want to stay in this room, but neither did I the other. I was in a bind, and one your establishment very much took advantage of. Where else would I have gone to at such a late hour? Forthwith, I write to inform you that I should like to be compensated for the full fee of such a stay, or I shall feel compelled to ruin you all over town.

I await with interest your response.

Yours faithfully,

Jane Austen

## *GRACE*

EMAIL
20.59
FROM: GRACE ABELLA
TO: CHARLOTTE BRONTË FAN CLUB
SUBJECT: RE: JANE AUSTEN LETTER

Dear Mrs Wilson and Erin,

Jinx. Here's mine. I can meet you after school tomorrow at a little café near me called *La Saison Sol* to discuss if you like?

Kind regards,

Grace

JANE AUSTEN COMPLAINT LETTER — GRACE

House Museum
Winchester Rd
Chawton
Alton, GU34 1SD
Eighteenth of May 1816

Ye Premier Inn
Ring Fort Rd
Cambridge, CB4 2GW

# To Whom It May Concern,

I write as a precursor to beginning legal proceedings, should you not respond in a manner I deem acceptable forthwith.

I had the great misfortune to stay at your ill-conceived excuse for an Inn, on the seventh of this month, Year of our Lord 1816.

I cannot be the first person to tell you it is illegal to let rooms that have a huge hole in the floor due to fire damage that has not been adequately repaired.

Had this night not been such a busy one, I would have gladly gone elsewhere, and did desperately try in vain to do so.

Happenstance led me back to your odious abode, and by sheer luck I was still alive in the morning, having not fallen through the gaping chasm.

Upon my word, this is unacceptable!

I enclose in this letter a bill to you, firstly to reimburse, and additionally to compensate me for the terror and danger I faced from my night in your calamity coven.

If I do not hear from you within 28 days, I shall begin legal proceedings. And I shall send around an inspector to check the hole has been adequately fixed.

Also, I am a famous author and I am not above reporting your hovel to the British press, should you attempt to countersue. If you vex me further, I will destroy you.

Yours faithfully,

Jane Austen

### ERIN

OK, I reluctantly agree she is good at stuff like this.

But I think I also might hate Grace. Actually hate her. I'm so angry, I don't think I even find her intimidating any more. It's just so unfair.

Grace is *so* two-faced. Not that this is in any way a surprise but OMG she was so horrible in English!!!!

And then she's all, "Oh here's my letter, let's meet up at my local café." Like WHAT. Just pick a behaviour, you absolute horror.

(Actually, slightly worried that Grace had overheard me say I didn't like her when I was fighting with Nicole, which might explain everything…)

Thank goodness Nicole and I are back to normal, though. And Theo and all my bullies are back to normal too. Ha. Aaaaarrggghhh.

Actually, Theo is calling me "Monster Mash" now,

instead of "monobrow", which I think is actually in part because Grace started saying that Nic and I live in *Little Shop of Horrors*.

Or it could be because I finally did a slightly better job of my eyebrows? Who knows? Who cares? What's a worse insult anyway?

One day I will leave this school and … be a dog walker. Or a journalist. Who knows? Who cares?

Maybe I will write scripts and move to L.A.?

Maybe I will die of wearing underpants that are too tight? I read somewhere that more people die of wearing underpants that are too tight than win the lottery. Actually, that doesn't sound right…

Oh, who knows! Who cares!

My point is – nothing matters.

Happy thoughts – woo – dinner = whole load of left-over mini-quiches, crisps, some slightly dried out carrot sticks, some mini vegetable samosas and mini onion bhajis, some grapes and some Twiglets.

I don't know who was in the meeting Mum stole all that from, but hats off to them for liking Twiglets but not enough to finish them. Please continue to make good life choices like that, because Mum won't buy Twiglets; she thinks they are overpriced for the nutritional value that they contain.

# CHAPTER TEN

**Wednesday 27th February**

*GRACE*

Hahaha. I was delighted to see Erin skulking around outside *La Saison Sol* looking awkward and out of place.

"Oh, I thought I'd got the wrong place," she said (instead of "hello") as I marched up to her. "It looks a bit... I mean... Are we even allowed in? Don't we need to *wear suits* or something?"

"Oh Erin!" I shook my head patronisingly and chuckled. "There *is* a dress code, but it's just no jeans or trainers. We're fine in our school uniforms." I moved towards the door.

"But still, shouldn't we go somewhere more...?

You said it was a *café*."

I rolled my eyes at her and entered the restaurant, so she had to follow me or look super chicken.

"Ah, Miss Abella," said the *maître d'*, recognising me. "Welcome back. May I take your coats?"

"What is your life?" whispered Erin, as we were seated at a nice booth.

I ordered some sparkling water for the table and our waiter promised to return momentarily to take our order.

"They've started doing a lovely afternoon tea here," I advised Erin, pretending to peruse the menu which she looked afraid to touch. "A selection of little sandwiches and tiny cakes, with a pot of tea," I explained. "Of course, the pastries here are to *die* for, because it's French. The coffee is marvellous too – goes without saying, really."

"I can't afford any of that stuff," said Erin.

"Oh. What can you afford?" I asked her.

"Tap water."

It probably sounds ridiculous, but it really hadn't dawned on me that Erin was … well, poor. Uncouth sure, with bad manners and an attitude. But I forget that such things often stem from other disadvantages.

I felt a small twinge of regret at that moment. But then I reminded myself that it's not *my fault* if Erin's parents make bad decisions and can't manage their money properly.

Still, I probably looked a bit tactless.

"OK. Well, maybe I could order a selection of some things and we could share—"

"Don't bother."

"No need to be rude. I didn't mean to embarrass you," I said.

"I think we both know that's not true," said Erin evenly.

All right, I *did* mean to embarrass her. But only with the atmosphere. Not about money.

"Well, what would you have ordered in a *greasy spoon*?" I asked her.

"I don't know. I would have put a quid towards some chips. I've got mints in my pocket. Look, I don't care. You've shown me how the other half live. Well done. Shall we just do the work we came to do?"

It was at this moment that our waiter returned. I thought fast and ordered a *bol de frites* and *des pâtisseries*, both to share.

"Just eat a quid's worth," I told her, when he'd gone. She didn't look amused. Our millionth awkward silence ensued.

"I think Charlotte Brontë would have liked this place," I ventured. "She spoke French and spent time in France."

"Pah," said Erin dismissively. "Charlotte Brontë famously thought London society was too showy and superficial, when she finally saw it. I think she'd have *hated* this place."

"Well, agree to disagree," I said, actually feeling a bit hurt. How had I ended up with egg on my face?

And Charlotte Brontë is *not* Erin's working-class hero. She's *my* genius. Mine. She had very high standards of manners and civility, which Erin can't begin to fathom or appreciate.

Erin was supposed to feel scared and intimidated. Not angry and righteous. I'm a bit confounded that my plan backfired.

"So I made some notes about your letter," said Erin.

"Great. Me too. About yours. Shall I start?" (I really thought I ought to be the one in charge of the situation.)

"OK." Erin leaned back in her booth seat and spread her hands in a gesture that was meant to imply *go ahead*, but actually came off as a bit sarcastic.

"Well," I paused. (Why was *I* starting to feel flustered?) "I think there was a lot of repetition actually."

"Oh really? That sounds like what I said to you last time."

"Well, it's true." I got her letter, which I'd printed, out of my school bag. "Look here, *most grievous experience, and I am most vexed* – repetition of *most*. *'Your host then showed me ... terrible smell did fill my nostrils then'*. Repetition of *then*. Repetition of *intimated…*"

"OK," said Erin. "I get it. I mean, you are allowed to use words more than once, but I get that I might have been a *bit* repetitive."

"Yes," I agreed. "And also, there's a lot of very flowery language."

"Excuse me?"

"Well, it reads a bit like you were just having fun and showing off how many fancy words you know."

"Well, I was. That was the exercise. Write in the

style of Jane Austen. We were *meant* to have fun with the style."

"No. The exercise was to write a letter of *complaint* in the style of Jane Austen. You should get to the point sooner. I mean, you were having *fun* the whole time. Even with the address of the hotel."

"OK," said Erin. "Notes taken. Have less fun. Shall we do you?" She reached into her bag and pulled out some paper.

"I like how you used real addresses," she began.

"Yes," I explained. "One is now the Jane Austen museum, where she lived for the last eight years of her life."

"The other is a real Premier Inn in Cambridge. Why did you pick on them?"

"Oh. Well, Daddy had to stay there once, due to a clerical error, and it was just awful. There were…" I leaned in and whispered, "…*bogeys* on the shower curtain."

Erin looked unfazed but replied, "Terrible."

"I guess he's just used to really amazing hotels," I said. "Do you have any more feedback?"

"Well. Just … you go in a bit strong. I mean, it's a bit aggressive. It reads like you were channelling real anger when you wrote this."

"Thank you." I was delighted. (Erin basically just said I was a brilliant writer.) "And also, you know, that's how you get results. Go in hard. Scare them. Make them take you seriously. Daddy taught me that."

"You can go too far, though. You're sort of using a sledgehammer to crack a nut."

"Thanks." I really liked this analogy and considered my aggressive words to be excellent hammers, that nuts would stand no chance against.

Our food arrived.

"Cool," said Erin. "Well, I guess we've done the assignment. See ya." She moved as if she was going to get up.

"No, no, please stay," I insisted. "Look. I apologise, OK? I *did* bring you here because I thought it would make you feel awkward. Please let me make it up to you by sharing some of this food. I'll never be able to eat it all myself."

Erin sat back down. She looked like she was really thinking this over, then she said, "Thank you," and took a *frite*. "Wow, these chips are amazing." She took some more.

"They are!" I agreed, relieved. "You have to try *les pâtisseries* too."

We tucked in and I poured us both tea.

"Should we talk about the elephant in the room?" asked Erin then.

"What's that?"

"Why?"

"Why?"

"Why did you want me to feel awkward? Why are you always picking on me? In English and, well, etc. etc."

"Oh." I was surprised she was acknowledging this. I wasn't quite sure what to say. "Well … because … you…"

(What was I going to say? *Because you don't like me?* Pathetic. I am not pathetic. Oh god. *Had* I been pathetic?)

I pulled myself together. "Look, believe it not Erin, you're not blameless. You've actually been quite rude about me too, you know. I've seen you and Nicole roll your eyes about my singing, and I heard you say you don't like me. At least I have the guts to say it to your face, instead of behind your back like a coward."

"*Oh*, you think you're not a *coward?*" She responded angrily with a dry chuckle. "So getting all your friends – if not the *whole class* – to gang up on me is *brave* is it? Theo has gone from calling me 'monobrow' to 'Monster Mash' because of you."

"Well, what is the deal with your eyebrows at the moment? Sorry – different issue."

"You're a bully," said Erin.

"All right look," I said crossly. "I want to *win* the Charlotte Brontë writing competition, OK? I don't like that you've come in out of nowhere and you're just taking all my stuff."

"Wow." Erin sat back and did some overly theatrical *I can't believe it* faces. "You've been making my life a misery because of…? Just wow. OK."

"I haven't been making your life a misery. *Have* I? I mean, you don't care what I say or do. You're the emo girl that doesn't care."

"*Why* do you think I'm emo?"

"You're really sarcastic and dowdy."

Erin actually laughs at this. "OK. Well, I asked."

"OK, look. I'm sorry, Erin. I'm sorry I've been unkind to you. I'll stop doing it. And I'll tell everyone else to stop as well."

Erin looked flummoxed. "Um. OK. I'm sorry if I've offended you with eye rolling and saying I didn't like you."

"Thank you," I replied graciously.

"So, I guess we're … friends now?" said Erin tentatively.

"Yes," I agreed carefully. "Cheers to that!" And we clinked teacups. "Actually, you know what," I said, suddenly remembering something. I put my cup down and pulled a flyer out of my bag. "Have you seen this? There's a Brontë play at the local Playhouse."

### ERIN

So much drama had already happened in the space of like ten minutes at that stupid posh restaurant, I couldn't think straight. We were *friends* now? And then suddenly the play … *WHAT?*

"Would you like to go with me?" asked Grace.

"Um … I'm not sure," I said. I thought of what Nic's face would look like when I told her.

"Why are you unsure?" demanded Grace. "This is a *brilliant*, on point, extra-curricular activity," she stated. Pretty convincingly.

Oh, who cares what Nic thinks.

"Let's do it."

Yeah.

# CHAPTER ELEVEN

**Friday 1ˢᵗ March**

*ERIN*

Grace has REALLY started being nice to me! It's been so weird!

When I arrived at the next English lesson, she stood up and said, "OK, listen up everyone! Guys, this is Erin and she's *actually* not that bad." (I mean, baby steps but yay. *Not that bad.*)

They all looked from me to Grace blankly and confusedly. Sylvie screwed up her face in a frown, then shrugged and said, "OK. If you say so."

And just like that, life was suddenly way easier.

When I told Nic I was going to see the Charlotte Brontë play with Grace she thought I was bluffing in a bid to convince *her* to go!

"Is this some kind of weird power play? I've *said* I'll go, if you pay."

"And I'm saying you don't have to."

"So are you besties with *precious Gracie* now?" she teased, but she seemed a little bit unnerved. And then she suggested going to the cinema together on Friday night.

The cinema is a luxury that I can't always afford, but luckily for me, our local cinema had some huge technical issues on the first night of the new Star Wars and everyone wanted their money back, but instead everyone got free tickets to see another film.

To cut a long story short, Kiera and I managed to find quite a few free tickets in *and* near the bins outside. So we now have a (limited) supply of film choices. We divided them up evenly and are very careful how we choose.

But anyway – woo – little Erin was out for the second Friday night in a row! (Incredible scenes.) Plus, I didn't need ear plugs for the cinema. Although they were still in my bag, just in case.

When Nic and I were queuing at the cinema, I was telling her about how much better English was now that I'm not being bullied all the time, but she seemed a bit distracted, and then I worried that I was offending her, so I quickly added, "Obviously it's still not as good as sitting next to *you*." I felt like a nice compliment might get her back onside.

"Oh, you're not still complaining about *that* are you?"

Honestly, I feel like I just can't win with Nic at the moment. If I say I have *fun* in English, she accuses me of being best friends with Grace. If I say I miss sitting with *her* in English, she tells me I should get over it. *What does she want from me?*

"It's hilarious really," I continued. "Did I tell you? Grace thinks we're dowdy! Just because we don't dress like identikit Barbie dolls! Like, we just look normal. But because everyone else is hyper into looks, we look dowdy by *default*."

"Did she say *you* were dowdy?" Nic asked. "*I* wear eyeliner. I doubt she thinks I'm dowdy."

"You're kind of missing the big picture here, Nic." (And Grace definitely *did* think Nic was dowdy.)

OK, to be fair, Nic is more stylish than me. She has dark brown hair, with this cool giant fringe, and her eyeliner does really make her eyes pop. And she's more confident than me. And more laid back. And kind of messes about more than me. But we have the same sense of humour. Nic would have laughed at the fake hotel address in my Jane Austen letter, I reckon.

I'm kind of pale. Pale skin, dark but sort of mousy brown hair. No fringe. Big forehead. Big visible eyebrows. Or at least ... even I don't know what's going on with my eyebrows at the moment.

Anyway.

"I said we'd meet Liz here," Nic announced.

"Who?"

"Here she is!" Nic beamed as Liz approached us. "You know Liz?" Nic glanced at me. "Sits with us in English? Well, sits with *me* in English."

"Sure! Hi, Liz!" I enthused, while secretly wondering why Nic didn't mention this sooner.

Was she *trying to make me jealous*?! Like, has she just invited Liz to make a point to me that she has other options? Or is this a genuine thing she thought would be fun?

"Hi, Erin. We miss you in English."

Should I be jealous of Liz, I wonder? I mean, I think Liz is nice. And I want my friends to be happy.

"Oh, don't miss Erin," said Nic lightly. "She's having loads of fun in boffin squad without us."

And then they proceeded to tell me all about how they have to keep getting into pairs and learn lines and practice a scene from *A Midsummer Night's Dream*, but they keep laughing because the words are so funny.

At first, I guess I was a *little bit* jealous, because it did sound sort of fun. But weirdly, as they talked, I discovered that actually I possibly felt happier to be missing it. Because like, sometimes the laughing can distract from the learning. Oh no. I *didn't* just think that. I am *not* turning into Grace.

We went into the cinema. They bought popcorn, but I cunningly had a peanut butter sandwich in my bag that I made at home. (I often try and side-step money issues by being very *Blue Peter* and eating things *I made earlier.*)

It's not like Liz and Nic were being horrible to me. (Apart from when Nic said about me, "Honestly, she's supposed to be *so clever*, but she can't even name *The Crumples'* first single!" and she and Liz laughed even though I'm pretty sure Liz doesn't know that song either.)

But apart from that.

They did include me and we had a laugh talking about lots of other things, not *just* things that happen in English.

We saw this really great, slightly spooky film about these teenagers in a haunted house, but nothing that bad happens.

Nic started a new WhatsApp group for the three of us. She called it "koolkidz&swot". That's fine. I don't mind. It will be fun.

I wasn't tired at all when I got home. (It's not like it was exactly *late*. My curfew is hardly conducive to being a night owl.) So I caught up a bit with this diary and then just lay on my bunk, thinking.

Kiera was on the sofa in the living room watching *Alexa and Katie* on Netflix and Mum was still out. I thought maybe I could have a quick stab at re-writing my Jane Austen letter, incorporating the changes Grace suggested...

I really had enjoyed that Jane Austen exercise. I don't care what Grace says. I *love* big flowery words. I love discovering a new word that perfectly describes something I want to say.

One of the times I re-read *Jane Eyre*, I made a list

of words that I didn't (previously) know. I got it out and read it through:

**Propitiate** – *to appease*
**Cicatrised** – *a scar over a healed wound, or on tree bark*
**Halitosis** – *a condition of bad smelling breath*
**Seditious** – *nearly treasonous public speech intended to promote disorder*
**Lachrymose** – *shedding tears*
**Pertinacious** – *tenacious, obstinate, unyielding*
**Phlegmatic** – *EITHER having a great deal of phlegm OR being of a calm, unemotional disposition*
**Splenetic** – *EITHER of the spleen, or bad-tempered, irritable OR melancholy*
**Diffident** – *lacking in self-confidence, excessively shy or modest*
**Bellicose** – *contentious, warlike*

I love that Charlotte Brontë knew and used all these words. She was so clever and inspiring. I want to start using words like these.

I am too *diffident*. I want to be less *diffident*. Ha. I have already started.

Way too many teachers at my school have *halitosis*, I reckon.

I smile at myself and sigh.

I don't really fit in anywhere at the moment. I mean, maybe I never fitted in, but at least I had Nic. And Nic and I were the same. Kind of. We had fun.

Now I'm *still* too silly and fun for Grace and *Top English*, but I'm starting to be too snooty and serious to enjoy Nic's company properly.

I wonder if Charlotte Brontë ever felt caught in the middle, and that's why she wrote *Jane Eyre*.

She was sort of caught in the middle of a class divide. She was educated, clever and talented, with such perceptive sensibilities, but because of money, she and her sisters kept ending up trapped into being governesses to horrible rich children.

I guess life just isn't fair.

And at least they got to be published. Before they all swiftly died.

Must. Stop. Being. A. Downer.

Nicole pops up on the new WhatsApp group she's created with some callback to the film and waaaay too many crying-with-laughter emojis. Liz immediately replies in kind. I send one crying-with-laughter emoji just to join in.

My phone pings 6 more times immediately.

I turn it off.

I make a start on the second draft of my Jane Austen letter. On a Friday night, woo, go Erin.

I write it, incorporating Grace's changes, but unable to not be sarcastic about it. I'm suddenly aware that I'm the only person I'm writing it for. I don't fit anywhere. Nic would have found the sarcasm funny, but she'd have no interest in reading this. And Grace *has* to read it, but thinks sarcasm is a bad quality.

But maybe it's *good* to write *just for me*? Maybe that's how I'll find out what I really want to write about?

There. See? I can be positive. I'm not *lachrymose*.

# CHAPTER TWELVE

**Saturday 2nd March**

*ERIN*
EMAIL
09.14
FROM: ERIN BROWN
TO: CHARLOTTE BRONTË FAN CLUB
SUBJECT: RE: RE: JANE AUSTEN LETTER

Dear Grace and Mrs Wilson,
Take Two. Suggested changes incorporated.
Best,
Erin

# JANE AUSTEN LETTER OF COMPLAINT — ERIN

Jane's House
Winchester
Hampshire, England
Twenty-seventh of January 1815

The Serious Inn
Sombre Street
Really Not Laughing Town
England

Dear Sir or Madam,

I do not wish to be seditious, but I must tell you that I had a most grievous experience at your Inn on my way to M—shire last week.

My allotted room stank dreadfully of the pungent miasma of death. It was the most noxious aroma I have ever had the misfortune to inhale.

It was like the very walls themselves were built of halitosis and decaying shellfish. I feel my nose is still cicatrised from the experience.

Furthermore, your host did nothing to propitiate me, and far from being lachrymose, was instead

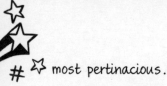

most pertinacious.

I am usually of a phlegmatic disposition, bordering even on diffidence, but I can tell you this episode has left me splenetic, edging toward bellicose.

I demand to be compensated for the full fee of my stay, and I should like also a letter of apology.

I await with interest your response.

Yours faithfully,

Jane Austen

## *GRACE*

EMAIL

10.26

FROM: GRACE ABELLA

TO: CHARLOTTE BRONTË FAN CLUB

SUBJECT: RE: RE: RE: JANE AUSTEN LETTER

Dear Mrs Wilson and Erin,

I haven't made any changes to mine because Erin said it was already brilliant. She said I went in strong and was using a hammer to crack a nut! What happens now?

Kind regards,

Grace

# Sunday 3rd March

EMAIL
20.58
FROM: MRS WILSON
TO: CHARLOTTE BRONTË FAN CLUB
SUBJECT: RE: JANE AUSTEN LETTER

Dear Both,
Well done! Let's meet at start of lunch on Monday (tomorrow) again, to discuss.
Best,
**Mrs Wilson**
*Second in Department for English*

# Monday 4th March

### *GRACE*
Had a wonderful Sunday lunch with Daddy at a Michelin-starred restaurant in London's Mayfair!

The great thing about living on the outskirts of London and the borders of the Home Counties is that one can just pop into "town" to do such things.

Everything is going pretty well at the moment:

Chloe is still happy with her new hamster; we're all going to go out next weekend – probably Saturday – and have dinner at Byron Burger, and then maybe have a sleepover at either my house or Sylvie's.

Erin and I are getting on OK too. My friends are usually pretty good at doing what I tell them (I'm kind of a great team leader that inspires loyalty that way). And Erin – to her credit – has been behaving much more normally herself.

Like, when she's not scared of us, she actually makes eye contact and answers questions without stuttering.

And she's *even* – dare I say it – quite *shrewd* and funny. She's actually made some insightful points in English, now that we're giving her a chance.

I've really turned her life around. I'm magnanimous like that. Giving other people a chance to shine.

Bizarrely, the only person not completely happy is Mrs Wilson. She seems to think that I didn't do the assignment properly by not making any changes at all. She thinks I misunderstood what Erin meant, and that "using a sledgehammer to crack to nut" is a bad thing! Like, it's unnecessary force, or something.

Poor Erin, using the wrong phrase to describe my writing!

### ERIN

I actually, in some ways, really admire how Grace is *so* confident that she will believe the earth is flat before she will believe you have insulted her. (And then at other times she is ridiculously sensitive.)

I mean, Mrs Wilson said she couldn't imagine Jane Austen using the phrase "I will destroy you", but Grace literally took that to mean she had a *better* imagination than Mrs Wilson!

To be fair, Mrs Wilson had lots of praise for both of our letters – she loved my use of flowery words, even if she thought they came slightly from out of the blue. (But when I explained about my Charlotte Brontë word list she was impressed.)

# CHAPTER THIRTEEN

**Thursday 7th March**

*GRACE*

Honestly, the *way* Erin reacted when I tried to take a selfie of us outside the theatre last night – you'd think she'd never seen a phone before! And the girl knows *nothing* about posing or angles.

She was all, "What are you even doing?" And when I explained, she seemed to think it's only appropriate to take selfies if it's *funny*. (Which actually would explain her insta feed.) She has no decorum.

And yet *she* had the nerve to be critical of *me,* and seemed to think *I* was the one being "*over-the-top*"!

I literally showed her how to do filters when we sat in the café before the play started. "How do you not know this stuff?" I was astonished.

She sort of sighed a bit sadly and said, "I guess I'm a rubbish teenager."

And then I felt bad. Even though it's not *my fault* if she has low self-esteem and a high level of online ignorance.

But because I'm magnanimous and kind I said, "Don't be silly," although I couldn't think of anything concrete to back that up with.

"I just … you know." She sounded weirdly wistful. "Sometimes I wish things were simpler. Can't we ever just enjoy a moment anymore? Charlotte Brontë didn't have to worry about social media."

I felt like she'd raised an interesting point. But the thing is, diary – we have NO WAY OF KNOWING how Charlotte Brontë would have reacted to the internet. Sure, it doesn't tally with her *nineteenth century persona*, but if she'd been born now, she might have loved it. And *therefore*, it is not for us to judge.

So, I put that thought in a box and decided not to try to even reconcile my two favourite things. No paradox for me today. No thank you.

And then I realised there *was* stuff that meant Erin

was *kind of* a cool teenager. "Isn't this a picture of you at a gig?" I pointed on my phone.

"Oh, *The Crumples*? Yeah."

"Is that a cool band?"

"Nicole thinks so."

I said that I thought there was something *exotic* about going to an intimate, dirty, grunge venue with a mosh pit. I'd only ever seen my favourite pop stars at the giant O2 Arena.

"Well, there you go then, I must be pretty cool," said Erin, laughing. Then she leant in. "Do you want to know a secret?"

"Always."

"I was wearing earplugs."

I spluttered incredulous laughter. She'd caught me off guard. But then she grinned, too. "Being cool can be very loud, Grace." And we chuckled.

Oh, and we both LOVED the play.

### ERIN

OK. Such weirdness!

I'm starting to find Grace really easy to talk to.

And Nic increasingly *hard* to talk to.

It's like they've swapped.

Nic mocks everything I say. And Grace has stopped mocking anything I say. I now live in opposite land.

Everything is sort of OK, though.

And I really enjoyed the Charlotte Brontë play. Though I was kind of embarrassed about Grace taking so many selfies. We got judgemental looks from the other patrons. Not that I should care.

Mum has even been stealing consistently good food from work. (They've had some coeliacs in for meetings and gluten-free food is much better than it used to be.)

So, it was about time some drama happened, and it happened today (Thursday).

Nic invited me back to her house after school AFTER Grace had already invited me back to *hers*!

We've been given a new English project (not just the CBFC) where we have to get into pairs and learn some of *A Midsummer Night's Dream*. (*Déjà vu* from Nic much?)

Anyway, Grace said, "Shall we just partner up? You can come to mine after school tonight and we can get ahead of this? I have a window and I'm usually very busy."

I think Sylvie and Brianna exchanged a slight look.

# But maybe I imagined that?

And then when I had to turn Nic down, she said, "I can't *believe* you're choosing *her* over *me*!" And I said I wasn't, but that Grace asked *first*. And Nic said, "*Oh ho*, I see how it is, don't worry." And then she stormed off.

## *GRACE*

Erin seemed really impressed that I get picked up from school in Daddy's car with my own driver. (*Adorable.*) She seemed shocked that I've never been on a bus. At least I don't think I have…? Can't remember anyway.

I think Erin was a bit surprised I'd suggested working together. But I just figured that if I chose the next cleverest person in the class, we'd definitely get the best grade.

I am not just a pretty face. And I am a *very* pretty face. (Not boasting – just practising self-love, babes.) #lovetoanyenemies

Erin is naturally bright and fast at memorising lines. Possibly a bit faster than me, but then I am busier than her in general, so I have more going on in my head.

I think Erin *thinks* she did a good job of not being too outwardly impressed with my house, but she could not stop gaping at it and I honestly felt a bit like I'd invited Oliver Twist to The Ritz.

I figured to stop it being distracting I'd give her the grand tour, but if anything that just made it worse. Maybe I should have dropped some of the historical points of interest and not mentioned the Jacobean staircase.

I made us both a snack. Well, I took the cold tapas that Mona had made earlier out of the fridge. (Mona is Daddy's housekeeper – sort of like a cleaner and chef, and she looks after me when Daddy's away.)

So, Erin and I sat at the high stools at the breakfast bar, in our contemporary kitchen, and I forced myself not to point out the Italian marble.

We decided to go to my bedroom to work, as Erin said the kitchen felt kind of too big and spacious.

"Wow," said Erin, appraising my room properly. "You have your own – wow, just so you know, your *en suite* bathroom is bigger than my bedroom."

"I don't know what to do with that information," I said.

"Fair enough," replied Erin, still looking around.

"Your bedroom is amazing. You're very lucky."

"Hashtag blessed," I joked, feeling even more awkward. "I'm sure your house is lovely too."

Erin actually laughed for about a minute then.

"It's a flat and it's more or less the exact opposite of this. Tiny and cramped, no privacy. I share a room with my little sister. Which is fine. Mainly."

"I'm sure I'd love it if I ever saw it," I said politely.

Erin chuckled. "Oh mate, you can never come to my house."

"None taken," I said primly, half joking.

"You don't want to come round. Believe me. Wow, look at your beauty corner! It looks like a vlogger's dream! I don't even know what half that stuff is."

"I can show you?" I offered. Erin nodded and gingerly approached my vanity unit.

I'm actually really into makeup and beauty at the moment. But all my friends are already well put together. Erin could actually be kind of a fun project…

"We will totally do our work in a minute," I began, "but do you want a makeover first?"

Erin grinned for a moment, then looked unsure. "I can't really … um… I get spots, I'm not sure I can really wear makeup, won't it make them worse?"

"OMG, you've come to the right place!" I enthused. "Yes – heavy foundation would *not* be your friend with acne, but light tinted moisturiser stuff, here…" I started getting out some products. "Bit of concealer…"

I looked up at her seriously. "And please, for the love of god let me fix your eyebrows!"

"You can … fix them?"

"Uh, *yas kween*!" I affirmed. "Is the Pope Catholic? Does Mr Rochester have a wife in the attic? *Of course* I can! I'm an *expert*."

Erin laughed and we sat down cross-legged on my plush wool carpet. I set to work.

"OK. Two things you need to know about eyebrows. One: your eyebrows are *sisters*, *not* twins, they are never going to look exactly identical and that's fine. Two: only pluck the stray hairs that come down, don't pluck the top of them or you'll end up with crazy shapes. OMG, you know what? I'm going to curl your hair!"

We still got all our work done. Obviously. But not before I turned Erin into a bona fide *snack* and instagrammed the whole thing. It was the most fun

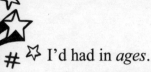

I'd had in *ages*.

"You look amazing!" I held up my oval, silver-framed mirror for her to see. "You should come out with us on Saturday!"

"Wow!" She was speechless.

I change lives. #lifechanger #itsagiftIhave

# CHAPTER FOURTEEN

**Friday 8ᵗʰ March**

*ERIN*

Well, I left Grace's house a *new person*. (Both physically and perspective-wise.)

OK, I'm not quite sure how I let Grace talk me into the whole makeover thing … except, she didn't really have to talk me into it *at all*. I had no idea I even *wanted* one.

Grace was weirdly so generous as well. She gave me loads of free samples that she doesn't need, and a few bits and bobs she says she doesn't use any more. I basically have a *makeup bag* now. *Me!*

It was bizarre to see that Grace has such a kind side, after everything that happened before. She must be lonely, I think. Spending so much time all on her own, rattling around in that giant house.

I actually felt a bit sorry for her. (Which I KNOW sounds insane.) Her house is incredible. She's super wealthy. She has literally everything a teenage girl could *possibly* want.

Well, not quite everything. I had half expected the tour to include the room she had written about in the *Three Bears* story, but it didn't. I felt like that room was there somewhere, though.

I have things that she doesn't: a mum and a sister. *I am fortunate.*

I complain a lot. But maybe I'm actually the lucky one? Maybe I should hug my mum and my sister and tell them I love them?

At least, that was what I was thinking until I got home and Kiera said, "Oh my god, nice hair! What happened? Did you get electrocuted?" And then laughed loads. Like, too much.

But I still *secretly* thought that I loved her, even then.

You know who agrees with Kiera, though? Nic. As I found out this morning in the form room.

"Um, are you feeling all right?" (This was her

version of "hello".)

"Yeah, why?"

"Cos it looks like you've had some kind of meltdown on insta." She held up her phone. "Why are you tagged in all these photos? Why is there a photo of you with your hair in rollers? What's going on with you?" She paused. "*We usually laugh at people who insta their hair appointments.*"

"Well yeah, but that was hardly a hair appointment. I was at—"

"I know where you were," she interrupted me. "And why are you suddenly fine with cutesy, unironic captions?"

"Eh?"

"'Thanks for sticking with me throughout this crazy journey babes! #blessed #goodvibes #whyareyousoobsessedwithme'."

"Well I didn't write that, but it's just a bit of fun," I explained. "And I think it's still a *tiny* bit ironic… Anyway, you said yourself I was dowdy. What's wrong with experimenting with different looks?"

"Uh, I didn't say you were dowdy. Your new best friend did."

"You said *you weren't* dowdy." I tried to remember it accurately.

"Yeah, so?"

"So, I don't want to be dowdy." I realised as I said it. "I'm allowed to do stuff, Nic. What do you care who I hang out with, anyway? You're making new friends, with Liz being everywhere all the time. Why can't I make new friends too?"

"Liz hangs out with you as well. You're always invited. We don't go off and do *secret* stuff behind your back."

"Mate, I went round to her house to learn *A Midsummer Night's Dream* lines. You *literally* did that with Liz. You can't be annoyed about it."

"I didn't insta my amazing transition to some stupid Barbie doll!"

Though Nic *did* insta a picture of her and Liz in front of a big advert for a donkey sanctuary at the bus stop with the caption, "Liz is an ass. Shakespeare innit mate #livingmybestdonkeylife", which I had thought was funny at the time. I even *liked* it.

"Look I can't win, can I?" I accused her. "If I say I *miss* you in English, you say I'm complaining and being negative. If I have *fun* in my new situation you get jealous. What am I supposed to do here?"

"I don't like you complaining because I'm sad you're gone!" Nic suddenly had tears in her eyes. "I'm sad too."

"Oh, don't cry, Nic!" I instantly felt terrible. Nic hardly ever admits she has feelings. She's almost always joking.

Liz appeared from nowhere, put her arm around Nicole and said accusingly to me, "Maybe you should just *go*."

So I did. Even though there wasn't really anywhere *to go*, because we all sit at the same clump of desks. I just went to the toilet and then came back. And felt like a weirdo.

# CHAPTER FIFTEEN

**Saturday 9th March**

*GRACE*
Decided to write a poem because I'm good at all
sorts of things.

> **I saw a bird**
> *I saw a bird*
> *From far away*
> *It looked so big like it might eat me*
>
> *I saw a bird*
> *Up close by*
> *It looked so small like it could barely fly*

*I saw a bird*
*It looked so sad*
*It looked so mad*
*It looked so bad*
*It looked so glad*

*I don't know what kind of bird you are*
*I don't know if we will travel far*

*Like a murder of crows*
*Or a muster of storks*
*A charm of finches*
*Or a kettle of hawks*

*A fall of woodcocks*
*Or a raft of ducks*
*A flight of swallows*
*Or a dole of doves*

*A parliament of owls*
*Or a party of jays*
*And are we going*
*The same ways?*
#nailedit

Thinking I should have a party soon! It's never not a good time to celebrate me, babes.

### Sunday 10th March

*ERIN*

Well, Nicole is *still* not speaking to me. *So immature.* Is there a word that means "feeling guilty, sad and angry all at once"? If there is, then I am it.

(In fact, side note: someone should invent an App that's like a thesaurus but does word combos like that? Note to future self: invent this please and become a millionaire.)

Anyway.

I was having *fun*. I felt *good*. I finally had some of that elusive *self-esteem* that I keep reading is very important for young people. I CAN BE GOOD AT DOING STUFF AND LOOK GOOD AND FEEL GOOD. What a revelation.

And now I suddenly feel all full of angst again, like I've done something terrible to Nicole, and I'm on shaky ground and wrong about everything.

And I hate it.

And now I've had a taste of feeling good, I'm

actually kind of annoyed with Nicole for taking my nice feeling away. And I don't even *want* to apologise to her.

I was so upset and frustrated that I decided to go against my gut instinct and do something crazy – I WENT OUT WITH GRACE AND HER FRIENDS.

I KNOW.

It was not my best decision. And very much a dumb move in terms of convincing Nicole that I am not a *basic Barbie*.

Not to mention, I still distrust and fear Grace's group of friends, and to a certain extent Grace herself.

Still, I made my eyebrows look good before I left so it wasn't like I hadn't made an effort.

And Sylvie even said, "Your eyebrows look really good now." (Without laughing, so she must have meant it.)

I said thanks, but there was still an awkward pause. So I said, and yes, I am cringing as I remember this, "Am I on fleek now?"

It was greeted by stifled (and in some cases not stifled at all) laughter.

"Uh, yeah, sure *Grandma*, you're *on fleek*," said Sylvie. And they laughed again.

"Stop it," said Grace. "You said you'd be nice."

"Sorry Erin," said Sylvie. "Give my regards to 2016. Sorry, last one. I promise. Sorry."

Grace was giving Sylvie evils, so Sylvie changed the subject. "Babe! Let's insta!"

They all instantaneously formed this kind of ludicrous pose. Grace put her arm around me, pulling me in. They did ridiculous pouts and jokey attitude faces, while Sylvie snapped away with her well-practiced selfie-arm, then said, "OK, let's do a funny one!" (Like none of those had been funny!)

They all agreed on their favourite and posted it.

I wondered how long it would be before Nicole saw it.

I pictured Nicole saying, "We laugh at people who insta their hair appointments, remember?"

I looked at the post online. They'd chosen a really terrible one of me, where I had my eyes closed.

Figures.

I watched Grace take a bunch more selfies in front of the poster of the film we were seeing, and genuinely started questioning my life choices.

Then she posted one: "So excited! Your girl is about to see the latest blockbuster! #outout #excited

#supportlocalcinema" (As if that's *even a thing*?!*)*

All I could think was SHE IS NOT A CELEBRITY. Why does she act like she is? And what am I doing here?


### *GRACE*

I looked really cute in that cinema pic. I was really happy with my hair, and I managed to get the exact right angle and everything. It got loads of likes too.

It was a shame Erin couldn't come back to mine afterwards. We all had so much fun! We ordered pizza and everything.

I've started a "New English" WhatsApp group (with no Chloe, sob) and added Erin. So we can still chat *to* Chloe/about Erin in the other group. And Chloe won't feel left out when we talk about lessons and stuff.

I mean, it wasn't really Erin's *fault* she got moved. She can't help being clever.

I wonder if that's why her friend Nic doesn't like her any more? Because she's so much cleverer than her? I expect Nicole must be quite insecure; no one wears that much eyeliner unless they're not trying to compensate for *something*.

Well, at least Erin has our new group, even if Nicole doesn't like her any more.

# CHAPTER SIXTEEN

**Monday 11ᵗʰ March**

*ERIN*

The "New English" WhatsApp group I've been added to is mainly indecipherable gifs from "cool girls" asking each other about homework and which boys are hot. I don't get all the references.

I felt nostalgic for Nic over-using crying with laughter emojis and berating me for not knowing all her favourite songs.

Kiera may have noticed I was down over the weekend, and I may have ended up telling her a tiny bit about it.

And she may have said that it sounds like neither friendship is perfect and that's OK because there's way more people in the world, and maybe I'll find my perfect friend in the future, or at university.

I don't know when she got so wise.

And she's wrong.

Nic *is* my perfect friend. Probably. Almost definitely. (Minor detail that she's not speaking to me, and is sometimes rude to me. I hear it.)

She has to be my perfect friend. I don't want to be the person with *no real friends*.

I sat next to Nic at Monday registration and she ignored me again.

So I messaged her a screen grab of the group insta picture at the cinema, and wrote, "If U want a laugh, and 2 C how beloved I am by the other Barbies, here is a pic."

She looked at her phone and snorted laughter, then, still not looking at me, she replied: "Nu phone, who dis?"

I laughed. Then we looked at each other and smiled.

"I'm sorry," I said to her face.

"I forgive you," she replied happily.

I was immediately irked. Why wasn't her reply

"*I'm sorry too*"?

"That picture is hilarious," said Nic. "They must really hate you."

"I think Grace might actually like me now," I replied. "But the others – no doubt. And they mocked my use of the phrase *on fleek*."

"Oh god." Nicole laughed and facepalmed. "Did you say *on fleek* in their company?" I nodded gingerly but grinned. "Oh, luv." Nic shook her head faux-compassionately. "This is why you should never say things without running them past me first."

I know she was joking, but I felt stung.

I'd had Nicole back as my best friend for less than *two minutes* and I already felt lonely again.

Is my eleven-year-old sister right? Do I secretly have *no real friends*?

"Well, listen," Nic said, "you can make it up to me properly by coming to mine for a sleepover soon and helping me crimp my hair."

MAKE *WHAT* UP TO HER?! She still hasn't apologised to me!!!!! And HOW is that different to Grace curling *my* hair?

*Don't say that*, my brain advised. *You'd enjoy*

*crimping Nic's hair. Don't get fixated with principles and upset her again.*

"Sorry, how is that different to Grace curling my hair?" I asked out loud.

"Duh!" Nic rolled her eyes. "Crimping is really retro and alternative right now. I'm not going to look like a *Barbie*, I won't be *on trend*. And I think I'll really stand out at the next Crumples' gig! Which by the way is soooooon! *Aaaand* – drum roll please," (she actually did a drumroll), "my parents said they'd pay for your ticket as an early birthday present for you. How cool is that?"

"Wow. That's really cool."

*That* was my reply.

I didn't have the guts to stick up for myself or tell her anything that she'd done that had upset me at all.

I wish I could say what was on my mind without risking a great big fall out.

I felt weirdly trapped and angry. And confused because I thought I should feel happy, and I did a bit, but I was still cross.

## Wednesday 13th March

*GRACE*
EMAIL
21.56
FROM: GRACE ABELLA
TO: CHARLOTTE BRONTË FAN CLUB
SUBJECT: GHOST STORY

Dear Mrs Wilson and Erin,
Get ready to be spoooooooooooooked! My ghost story is attached.
Best,
Grace

## The Secret Room
*By Grace Abella*

Everyone had always assumed that Mary Miller was a good girl. She had all the characteristics that would indicate this was the case. Mary was shy and polite, and, if anything, a little diffident.

Mary worked in the factory and brought home her wages to her father and did as she was told. She

cooked the meals and kept the house and looked after the chickens and the dog.

No one would have suspected her of *anything*.

Sarah Juniper was a *different* story. She was loud, opinionated and sometimes swore. She lived alone with her cat in her cottage in the woods, since her father had died. No one had ever liked or trusted her. There were occasional whispers that some believed her to be a witch. But she was an excellent seamstress and so she continued to be given work in the village, despite her unpopularity.

Mary and Sarah became acquaintances at the factory, and then friends. Mary helped to make the fabric that Sarah would go on to sew. It was an unlikely pairing, and no one understood what either got out of it. The villagers just hoped that Mary would be a good influence on Sarah.

When the first child went missing, there was a huge hunt, and everyone went looking. Nothing was found, not even a body, and everyone feared that wolves or bears must be responsible.

When the second child went missing, a chill set in over the village and everyone became very afraid. Children were ordered to stay in groups of three or more.

At the third missing child, the sense of dread hung like a cloud over them. A curfew was introduced, and men from the village started patrolling in vigilante shifts, in order to try and protect those remaining.

And then the whispers started. And the whispers turned into a murmur, and the murmur turned into a *roar* that Sarah Juniper must be responsible – SHE MUST BE A WITCH.

And so they marched on Sarah Juniper's cottage in the woods. And they found a *locked room* with four beds containing the three children, asleep but alive.

Sarah seemed to be in a funny state where she couldn't remember things. She claimed she was trying to help *save* the children, but she wasn't able to explain from whom.

So the villagers hanged Sarah from the tree outside her own cottage on suspicion of being a witch and of kidnapping children.

The children were brought home but could not be woken up. A call went out to find a physician from another village that could help. The men stopped patrolling the village and instead went hunting for assistance.

Everyone thought everything would get back to normal once they could just get these sleeping children to wake up. The witch was dead. It was all going to be fine.

AND THEN

A *fourth* child went missing.

AND THEN

The *first three* children disappeared again.

The villagers searched Sarah Juniper's cottage from top to bottom, and the surrounding area, but to no avail.

*No one* thought to look in Mary Miller's house. No one thought to look in her attic where she kept her spell book and four beds with four sleeping children in them.

And no one noticed as the years went by that Mary Miller didn't age.

Until one day, twenty years later, on the anniversary of Sarah Juniper's hanging, there was a fire.

No one knew how it could have started, but it looked like a candle had somehow fallen on to a giant book in the attic. One person said they saw a cat leaping out of a small attic window, moments before the blaze took hold.

When the villagers put out the fire, they found four sleeping children – unharmed and unaged in the attic – and the burnt body of an elderly woman who looked a bit like Mary Miller.

Legend has it that once a year, on the anniversary of her death, the ghost of Sarah Juniper can be seen walking through the village, noose still around her neck, holding her cat.

# CHAPTER SEVENTEEN

**Thursday 14ᵗʰ March**

*ERIN*

Oooh. *Chills*. A bit.

But more importantly – Grace used the word *diffident*! She totally must only have used that word after I was talking about my word list last time. She *never* used it before then.

I am *spreading words*! (I am an actual writer!) I am improving literacy, haha – for *Grace* of all people.

Oh man. Grace's ghost story is good, though. (Though it's got weird similarities with a few other stories – not least *The Picture of Dorian Gray* by Oscar Wilde.)

But she's still made it different and quite tense and full of suspense *and* still have a good twist. Grace is really good at twists. *I* should do some twist endings…

I only have a vague idea of what to do for mine. Aaaagghhh.

### *GRACE*

OK. I am definitely going to have a party!!!!!

Daddy has green lit my new venture. (I have ace negotiation skills babes.)

I see this as a practice run for a Sweet Sixteen Party (which is still like, a year and a bit away BUT practice makes perfect). And it can't hurt to start finding out who all the best caterers are now, can it?

Plus, if I get Daddy used to the idea of pushing the boat out now, incrementally, it won't seem so outlandish when I tell him the full scale of my plans for then. #alwaysthinking

And it's just fun to dress up and stuff.

I invited Erin when we were practising our Shakespeare at my house, and I've told her she can bring a couple of friends if she wants to. I think her and Nicole have made up again. I can't keep track, too much *drama*. (But not everyone can be as healthy and well balanced as me, babes.)

### Friday 15th March

*ERIN*

I'm going to a mad-sounding party!

There's going to be an ice sculpture, and a giant piñata, and (according to Grace) a snow leopard on a leash. That can't be true. And seems cruel. And my mum definitely would not let me go if there was a wild animal there. Of course it's not true. Is it?

Anyway look, OK, I officially don't care about stuff like parties, because Nic and I are above it. And we don't follow the herd and all of that.

But also, Grace's parties are kind of legendary at our school. And it's not like I ever tried to become her friend so I could go to one, but I am excited that it has still happened.

I had fun with Grace practising Shakespeare at her house.

Had the most bizarre conversation with her actually. She's so confident. I don't get it. It's baffling.

Why isn't she filled with debilitating and crippling doubt like the rest of us?

I was telling her how I don't really get on that well with boys and that all my friends tend to be girls, like Nic. And she goes, "Yeah, I don't have any male friends either."

And I said, "*What?* The boys all *love* you. You're always exchanging *bantz* with them in the corridors. And they're always trying to get your attention."

And she goes, "OK. Let me re-phrase that: I don't have any male friends that *haven't tried to get off with me.*"

I mean, just *wow*, right? Talk about boastful. *Humblebrag much?*

But I said, "Oh ... really?" In a nice way.

She nodded. "I *know*, terrible, isn't it?"

"Um, yeah. It *is* terrible," I agreed. (Or would be if it was *true*, I thought.)

Grace continued, "I know. Like, *what*? They think they can just be talking to you one minute, about *nothing*, and then suddenly put their arm around you the next? It's like, ew, get off! Get over yourself already! I mean, *why are they always trying to get off with us?*"

I pictured Theo shouting "monobrow" at me, with the mime action for (I assume) "eyebrow" that he'd added. And then shouting "Monster Mash" (with no mime, *so far*).

I mean, they weren't *always* trying to get off with us. Hurling abuse was also in the mix.

"Uh … yeah," I said carefully.

I couldn't picture this problem happening to me. Which was GOOD. Because non-consensual grabbing is actually a crime. Even if it was someone nice, like Nick Brooker… Well, maybe not if he put his arm around me *very gently*, and checked I was OK with his arm before he left it there…? Maybe I'll Google the letter of the law on that.

"The entitlement," Grace was saying.

"*Yeah*, the *entitlement*," I quickly agreed. "Boys thinking you're *attractive*. We've all been there. Why can't they just … never reach out for human affection?"

"Right!" Grace nodded. "Exactly. It's the entitlement," she repeated.

"The entitlement," I parroted sagely.

Though it seemed vaguely ironic to me that Grace, of all people, had issues with people showing entitlement.

"And don't you just hate it," continued Grace, "when they lunge at you and you have to fight them off like dogs? Haha!"

Now, that is *definitely* a crime. That's full on assault. They're not supposed to be allowed to do that. Grace is *right* to be upset by this, it turns out. Why was she laughing so cheerfully about it?

"Yes," I agreed blindly. "I would h – I mean I *do* hate that."

No one has ever lunged at me. And I'm *glad*. Obviously. I think I would definitely find it obnoxious and scary.

But like … *should* I have been lunged at by now? Is it a rite of passage or something? Like when that supply teacher got told everyone's names wrong? Or maybe that's hazing. Is *hazing* a rite of passage?

And is lunging the only option? What about some nice, good old-fashioned, totally *consensual* handholding? (With say, Nick Brooker?)

I think me and Nick *might* have had another moment in music – or he could have just been squinting because of the sun. (I squinted back to join in, before I realised the sun wasn't really in my eyes.)

But why are the two options for interacting with boys either name-calling for failing to meet the apparent standards of beauty expected, or physical attack for exceeding them?

I guess if I had to choose between physical assault and verbal assault, I'd probably stick with verbal assault. So maybe I'm fine as I am?

I mean, frankly, the last thing I need right now is some *large-adult-son-in-the-making* lunging at me unannounced. I just don't want that kind of hassle. Why is Grace so sunny about everything and laughing off assault?

## Saturday 16th March

### *GRACE*

As you know, diary, I am completely happy in my own company, and very self-sufficient. I'm not one of those people who dreads to be alone with their own thoughts because they secretly hate themselves and need to distract the voices. Sure, I keep *busy*, but that's because I'm a go-getter (not because I'd otherwise be prone to bouts of depression).

Therefore, I think it's *great* to have a night in and

relax, recuperate, have a nice bath, maybe do a face-mask, practise *self-care* and catch up on my reading. I am absolutely *not* ashamed to be home, alone on a Saturday night. In fact, I cherish it.

So there I was, having a lovely time, *après mon bain moussant*, just sitting up in bed, reading *Jane Eyre* again and (obviously) occasionally checking my phone.

I knew Sylvie and Brianna and a couple of the others were going to go roller-skating, and I wasn't jealous at all.

In fact, it had been my idea, but I wanted to go *next* weekend, after a certain important netball match was out of the way, just in case I got injured.

I did say, "You could go this weekend, but then I can't come, or next weekend, and I can." But I suppose, if I'm honest, I was sort of bluffing. I didn't think they would actually go without me.

But it's fine. It's fine. I wasn't jealous, and anyone who says I was is mistaken.

Although (even though I wasn't jealous), I did feel a little bit sad every time I clicked on insta and saw another story of them whizzing round together. And they did some very cute posing by the huge,

cool neon sign that looked quite arty, and I realised I would have liked to do that.

But I am a *serious athlete*, treating netball with the importance and respect it deserves. I'm sure it's what Charlotte Brontë would have done, if roller skates had existed in the olden days and she was supposed to play netball at a high level like myself.

Plus, it was a good opportunity to do more party planning.

Obviously I checked my phone a bit, now and then.

Had a quick look at what Erin was up to.

I remembered her insta page as being all a bit zany and unkempt. But I guess I hadn't really concentrated properly.

There was a picture of her and (presumably) her sister, as little kids, next to a picture of them now, with the caption, "Slightly worried we still dress like this" because they were wearing the same colour tops and trousers.

It made me smile, but it also struck me as odd, to post a picture online and draw attention to being *unfashionable* in it, rather than, you know, emphasising how good you look.

But that seemed to be a recurring theme of Erin's

insta. She was always trying to be the butt of the joke and put herself down for a laugh.

She, and sometimes her sister, but mainly Nicole, were generally pulling comedy poses that were actually quite unbecoming – aesthetically speaking. It was like she didn't even *want* to look cute *at all*.

Erin currently seemed to be having loads of fun at a sleepover where they were dressed up as animals. She was a zebra, Nicole was wearing a leopard onesie, and this other girl was either a grey mouse or a koala or something.

There was a *SingStar* on in the background and a couple of stories of them variously dancing, singing and putting way too many sweets in their mouths, then gurning to the camera with loads of fizzy wands hanging out. Then Erin crimping Nicole's hair.

So many times, I thought, "I would never have posted a shot like *that*, so close to my nostrils," etc.

Then one picture really caught my eye. In it, Nicole must have said something funny because Erin was *really* laughing. She was laughing so much she had a massive double chin, and it was an unflattering angle, but she looked *so happy*. Carefree even.

And then I realised that's how she looked in all the

photos. She was either pulling a funny face that she didn't care looked ugly, or a wry sarcastic knowing face about whatever she was mocking, or she was just genuinely head back, snorting with laughter.

It took me another a moment to realise that I didn't feel judgemental or jealous, I felt ... wistful. Erin was free in a way that I – with my carefully, artistically crafted aesthetics – was not.

Erin could genuinely dance like no one was watching. Whereas *I* could do the perfect version of what it would look like if you were dancing like no one was watching, but were in fact very aware that actually everyone was, and you needed to make sure you still looked cute.

But so what? So sue me. I *care* about appearances. Because actually, appearances *are* important.

One *should* always be well dressed and appear tidy and clean and smart and competent. Daddy wears amazing suits because he believes the saying "clothes maketh the man" has truth to it.

One *should* think carefully about every picture one posts online because it could somehow affect a job interview when you are twenty-five. That's not excessively stressful, it's just *prudent*.

And actually, how do I know what Erin is thinking in these photos? She might think she looks great and super cute … though I doubt it.

And what if *she* is just *pretending* not to care? What if this whole account is a carefully-crafted attempt to look emo and not bothered about being beautiful? Looking breezy and insouciant?

Ever since Erin came into my life I've been full of questions and doubts and I don't like it. But I *think* I like Erin. I just worry she might be bad for me.

# CHAPTER EIGHTEEN

## Sunday 17th March

*ERIN*
EMAIL
16.47
FROM: ERIN BROWN
TO: CHARLOTTE BRONTË FAN CLUB
SUBJECT: RE: GHOST STORY

Dear Grace and Mrs Wilson,
Hope you've had nice weekends. My ghost story is attached.
Best,
Erin

# The Haunted Walk
## *By Erin Brown*

She'd been followed for at least thirty minutes now. She was sure of that. Thirty careful minutes that she'd made sure she didn't go any faster than she needed to.

Every time she crossed the road, he crossed the road behind her. Every time she turned a corner, he turned a corner behind her.

Thirty minutes. She stuck carefully to her speed.

Keep up the pace – *don't* do anything sudden or unexpected. *Don't* let on that you know … then maybe you'll still have the element of surprise…?

Keep to the well-lit areas. Take the long way around because there's more people that way.

At least there should have been. Where *was* everyone? Had everyone gone home early today? Why was there hardly anyone around? Did they know something she didn't? Or was fear making her paranoid?

It was getting darker and darker. Dusk had shape shifted into night-time like a fire turning into smoke.

Shadows loomed large everywhere. Streetlights were few and flickering.

All the shops were now shut. But there should still have been people. People like her, on their way home, on their way to their cars, to safety. To safety.

The march of the feet behind her continued their pace. Following her.

He was keeping his distance. For now.

What if he knew she was already far too alone? What if he knew already that he could make his move easily?

Why were there so few people around? She needed to keep to the light. But there wasn't enough light.

Should she tail around and go back? Back to the light? Back to the busyness and hubbub of the city centre? Back to the people? The shops were shut but the restaurants and bars and cafes would be open... There must be people there.

She could find help ... call a taxi ... find a policeman.

Would it be suspicious at this late stage? *Too suspicious* to turn around and double back?

Would that signal that she *knew*? He'd know he'd have to make his move soon...

But then… What if it was already too late? Her heart beat fast in her chest…

Was this it?

Should she run? Phone the police?

Suddenly she realised she couldn't hear the footsteps any more.

What did *that* mean? Had he gone? Stopped?

Should *she* stop? Turn around and see what was happening? Or just *run?*

She turned around.

The man was standing still, holding a gun.

"Get down!" he yelled at her. "*Now!*"

She ducked to the floor.

A new sound – padded footsteps getting nearer, faster. A great wolf-like creature leapt into the air above her.

The gun went off. Once, twice, three times.

The animal made a roar that turned into a scream and crash-landed in a bleeding heap in front of her.

The man approached, gun still aimed.

"You saved me!" she cried. "I thought you wanted to hurt me, but you wanted to save me from that wolf."

"I saved you from that wolf," he said, putting his

gun away, "so that I could drink your blood!"

He grinned and she saw his vampire fangs, growing in the flickering light.

**GRACE**

Ooooh, Erin finally did her ghost story. (Well, assuming "ghost story" as a category is allowed to include "*general Halloween stuff*"? I guess vampires are *technically* ghosts as they are dead…?)

It's a good story, though. Quite tense. (Though maybe not as tense as mine?) And it has *two* twists. Mine only has one really. Grace is getting good at twists. I wonder if she is copying me? Haha.

#everyonecopiesme #theycanthelpitbabes #iamthebest

EMAIL
17.58
FROM: MRS WILSON
TO: CHARLOTTE BRONTË FAN CLUB
SUBJECT: RE: GHOST STORY

Well done again both!

Shall we meet at start of lunch on Monday (tomorrow)

again, to discuss? Is this a good time to meet? When we make the group official we will need to stick to one lunchtime a week. Don't have to decide now. Have a think about which days will work.

Best,

**Mrs Wilson**

*Second in Department for English*

## *GRACE*

EMAIL

18.50

FROM: GRACE ABELLA

TO: CHARLOTTE BRONTË FAN CLUB

SUBJECT: RE: GHOST STORY

Dear Erin and Mrs Wilson,

Just to flag up I do have netball practice some lunchtimes. And as you know, I do lots of extra-curricular activities, so I think we should be mindful of that going forward.

Kind regards,

Grace

## *ERIN*

*Mindful?*

Not long ago that would have made me eye roll and text Nic about how annoying and pretentious Grace is.

Now it makes me chuckle affectionately.

Yikes.

But Grace doesn't *mean* to sound so officious. She just sometimes has crazy paranoia that everyone won't think she's important all the time.

Sometimes I think she's happier than me because she seems so confident and at ease with herself. Other times I think it would be exhausting being her, and I am better off because I don't care about stuff like if I am seen as important.

Like, I would never want to throw a big party like Grace. (And not *just* because my flat is so cramped that I can only really invite two people round at a time before it violates health and safety regulations.)

I would genuinely find it stressful trying to make it good and I'd hate it if everyone said it was rubbish. I just wouldn't find that fun. Grace loves all that. Like she thrives on that kind of stress. It's some fun challenge to puzzle-solve and perfect.

Not for me, no thank you. I don't need a big party.

I'm fine. I'm *happy*. Ish. I'm definitely happi*er,* though, I think.

I'm a bit worried I'm being two-faced about Nic though.

Grace explicitly said I'm allowed to invite Nic and Liz to the amazing party. And I haven't mentioned it to them yet.

I just sat about having fun at Nic's impromptu sleepover, eating her sweets and not inviting her to a cool party. Like a terrible friend.

I know I'm a hypocrite, but honestly, if Nic thinks that wearing a onesie while you insta a new hair-do makes it somehow subversive and ironic, then she is kidding herself and is a total hypocrite too.

I mean, I guess, maybe it is a *tiny* bit subversive. But *still.* In some ways, the irony only seems like a smokescreen, to hide that you actually secretly want to insta hair appointments. (I might be over-thinking this.)

Sometimes, now, when Nic is rude to me, I feel this weird anger flare up inside me; then I squash it back down and add it to the little ball of annoyance in my stomach where I keep my feelings about Nic at the moment.

I'm not sure this is a good long-term plan.

And it occasionally results in Nic going, "What's wrong? Are you annoyed with me?" as if she actually cares.

But then I go, "No, I'm fine."

And she goes, "Phew, I thought for a minute you were going off me because I can't recite pi to a hundred decimal places or whatever."

And then I go, "That's maths, not English."

And she goes, "So?"

And then I can't be bothered to point out that she's bullying me for being good at the wrong thing. Because that just proves I'm a swot even more. Or, you know, someone who pays attention to details.

Maybe I should say, "Don't call me a swot. It's hurtful and you've said it so much, it isn't funny anymore. And please change the name of that WhatsApp group."

But I know she'd just say, "I'm only joking! Why can't you take a joke? God, I can't say anything to you any more, can I? Don't worry, I'll never say anything funny to you ever again!" Or something.

I mean, that's what she says in my head. And I'm usually right about stuff like this. So there's no point giving her a chance to prove me wrong. Because if I'm right, it will be an awful row.

My point is: it's just better to not confront.

# CHAPTER NINETEEN

**Monday 18<sup>th</sup> March**

*GRACE*

Well, today was a game of two halves.

The morning was fine. Caught up with all my friends. Chloe is worried her hamster is getting too fat. (*Honestly*. Eye roll emoji.) It shouldn't be *that* difficult to give a *hamster* proper nutrition.

That girl is a little more foolish than I realised. Not that I'm judging her as stupid just because she went down in English. I'm not a snob. (Well, only a tiny bit.) But it is weird how I never noticed before that she is not the sharpest tool in the shed.

#notjudging #lovetoanyenemies

Anyway. Had a lovely time in CBFC at lunchtime,

discussing our ghost stories.

Erin brought up an interesting point (which actually stemmed from something interesting *I* said – *just saying*).

Erin was *critiquing* my work, and said she couldn't tell what *ye olden* century it was set in as it was all a bit vague, and I should maybe give a clue or indication of a more specific era.

And I said, "Oh, you mean mention who the monarch is? Or have someone use like carbolic soap or whatever as clues?"

And then Erin said, "You know what I've always wondered? When you read a novel from *nowadays* that's set in the *olden days*, say the Victorian era – the characters will often refer to their soap as carbolic soap. So that we, the reader, are picturing how different soap was then, or it conjures a certain historically accurate image, etc. But like, in *Jane Eyre*, Jane only ever calls soap, *soap*. She never mentions if it's carbolic or not. Is that because she had regular soap? Or is it because ALL the soap was carbolic soap, and so there was no need to mention it?"

"That is a very interesting question," said Mrs

Wilson, looking impressed. "Although carbolic soap *is* a Victorian invention, it went with the whole Germ Theory Revolution pioneered by people like Joseph Lister. *But* the mass production of carbolic soap didn't happen until towards the end of the Victorian era, so Charlotte Brontë would most likely *not* have had it. She may well have had access to Pears soap, invented by Andrew Pears, though you had to be quite well-to-do.

"But it's great that you're thinking like a writer, Erin, and really trying to *picture* the accurate world your characters would inhabit."

I didn't even feel jealous that Mrs Wilson was giving Erin praise. I was pleased to have facilitated such a great bit of discussion. I'm very gracious and basically the *instigator* of *all* interesting things.

Then Mrs Wilson said maybe the two of us should meet up another time to discuss a bit more before we wrote our feedback notes.

"I don't mind coming to yours," I offered to Erin, after Mrs Wilson left. "If that's easier for you?"

"You can't come to mine," said Erin. "You wouldn't *fit*. Literally as well as figuratively. My flat is the size of this sofa."

"Well that's palpably not true," I replied.

Erin smiled at me curiously, then said, "I kind of want you to come round, just to see the horrified look on your face. But still no." She grinned at me.

I attempted to return the smile, but I'm not sure it passed muster. Truthfully, I felt a little put out. I'm not used to being told "no" very often. (Not because I'm *spoiled* – but because I'm a fantastic negotiator. Obvs.)

But still, I'm not used to being refused in such a manner.

Maybe this minute act of hostility was the tipping point for my otherwise pleasant morning, because the day certainly went downhill from there.

I joined my friends for the rest of lunch, and there were one or two unkind jibes about Erin. Then Sylvie said, "Shhh, Grace loves her now, remember."

"Oh, right yeah, the novelty still hasn't worn off yet then?" said Brianna.

"What novelty?" I asked them.

"Slumming it with a freakazoid," said Brianna. "You got it out of your system yet?"

"We thought you'd be bored by now," chimed in Sylvie.

I was too stunned to speak for a moment.

"I thought she seemed all right at the cinema," said Chloe unassumingly.

"Oh *Chloe*," said Sylvie mock-affectionately. Then she put up her hand in that attitude way, and went, "*Ya basic*."

Brianna giggled.

"I am *not*," said Chloe.

"Yes, you are," said Brianna. "And FYI, instagram does not need any more pictures of your stupid hamster."

"Hey," said Chloe.

"You should be more annoyed than *us*," said Sylvie. "You're the one she's *replaced*."

I couldn't believe what I was hearing. (Even though I had previously said lots of similar things myself.) I really thought they'd *listened* to me when I'd told them to be nice. But they hadn't properly taken it on board.

This was a blow. To my authority, my sense of who my friends were, *and* my place in the world.

Erin *wasn't that bad*. Why couldn't they see it?

Why didn't the *empirical evidence,* that she was *kind of a laugh* in English, not offset her former status as pariah more effectively? And why was I being *questioned* about my decisions?

I rallied. *No*. I will *not* be undermined in this way.

I am an *inspiring leader*. I am popular enough to survive *anything*. I am an excellent negotiator and an expert at human psychology. So I knew just what to do.

"No. *Ya basic*." I did the hand gesture and pulled my best *attitude* pose.

They looked at me affronted, so I continued. "Why are you being so *extra*?" I accused. "*God,* you two must be *so bored* if you think this is interesting enough to be a problem. Is everything all right *at home*?" I added patronisingly. Chloe sniggered.

"Look, granted, you fixed her eyebrows." Sylvie put a hand up placatingly.

"She does *look* a bit better now," Brianna agreed slightly sheepishly.

"But *come on*, Grace," Sylvie said. "Real talk. What's going on? You hated her. Why do you love her so much now?"

"I don't love her so much. *Babes*, I'm Switzerland

over here. Neutral as it gets… It's you who has no chill over there in *The Republic of Salty*."

Chloe suddenly got her confidence back, chortled, and said, "Ohhh, SNAP."

I pressed my advantage. "But, like, seriously, what was the bit about her that annoyed you?" I continued. "The bit where she lent you her pencil sharpener in English, or the bit where she was funny and insightful about Shakespeare and made our lessons more fun? Are your gold shoes too tight as well?"

"No, I just –" Sylvie was backpedalling like mad.

*"Oh my god,* are you *jealous*?" I crowed. "Is *that* what this is? Are you jealous I've got a new friend whose eyebrows I fix? Do you want me to do your eyebrows?"

"No," Sylvie replied, defeated.

"OK good," I said. "Then maybe stop being a thirsty little whiner."

"Sorry," said Sylvie.

"Yeah. She's not that bad," Brianna conceded.

(Yesss. I WON. Natch.)

"And so what if she's a bit fugly?" she continued philosophically. "You just look hotter standing next to her."

"That's true," said Sylvie.

I was just doing a victory lap in my head when Sylvie added, "She's all right in *English*. But, is she really coming to your party? And like, maybe we should *all* have a say in who comes out with us as a group? In the future."

I had to really fight not to show how shocked this made me. It was so out of the blue. Was Sylvie making a power grab? Even after I'd put her back in her box so magnificently?

And what could I say? I couldn't say, "No, *I'm the leader* and I decide everything." Not least because that's an *informal* title I've given *myself*. And also, I shouldn't *have* to *say* I'm the leader. It should just be obvious.

I went in for the attack, and I went in *hard*, and regained my position as the dominant one. Just like Daddy taught me. Why didn't it work? *Am I losing my skills of negotiation?* First Erin says I can't come to her house. Now this.

"Babes, she's coming to my party and it's all fine. So you can stop wasting my time with this pointless drama."

Sylvie shrugged her capitulation. But I felt vaguely

unnerved that the matter wasn't fully resolved.

Well, great. This is just great. Now I have to worry about future mutinies.

## CHAPTER TWENTY

**Monday 18th March**

*ERIN*

OMG. Nick Brooker has *followed* me, *liked* two of my Instagram posts, and written "LOL" under one of them!!!!!

THIS IS UNPRECEDENTED!!!!

He liked the one of me with Grace and her gang outside the cinema, where I have my eyes closed. (To be fair, that's probably what he thinks I really look like, what with all my weird squinting in music.)

Then he liked one of me at Nic's sleepover, dressed as a zebra, trying to juggle satsumas. And he wrote "LOL" under it. I think he really *gets* me.

WHAT DO I DO?!

I followed back and peeked at his insta. Then I liked a couple of his pictures (Nick standing with some friends, holding a football, and stroking a cat in a book shop).

Should I write something on the cat picture? Like "LOL cute"? Or "What the hell book shop is this?" I can't decide.

I screen-grabbed and WhatsApped Nic the pic of his "LOL" comment under my juggling photo, and wrote "Uh, I think I'm smoking hot dressed as a zebra maybe?" with some laughing emojis.

She immediately replied, "Oooooooooh! Not bad. But U can't date someone with the same name as me tho."

*Dating?* Ha! I mean who said anything about dating? OMG imagine if we started dating?!

NEW MESSAGE!

OMG.

Nick Brooker has private messaged me on insta:

"U goin 2 party? Winkyface, confetti canon"

I counted to one hundred and then replied, "Yeah probs. C U there? Music note"

He replied with a thumbs up!!!!

OMG who *even am I*?

I need to ring Nic and discuss what this means immediately!!!

But then I will have to tell her about the party.

Which I *should* do.

I was going to invite her eventually, though, wasn't I?

I will. *Soon.*

And I'll just have to give *myself* advice in the meantime.

### Tuesday 19th March

*GRACE*

Erin was acting kind of weird when she came round to mine after school. She'd started using some of the other makeup I gave her and she kept suggesting we take selfies.

I was still worrying about my friends' mutineering (need to check if that's the right word? It probably is. I'm usually a genius).

So I was really in the mood to *work* rather than do any more impromptu makeovers or insta stories, and therefore was a bit grumpy and kept saying no.

"Shall I do a story of us working?" Erin asked,

sounding excited. "What shall we say?"

"No. *What?* Look…" Then something clicked and the penny dropped – Erin's makeup, the breathless excitement, caring about insta – it could only mean one thing.

"Is this about *a boy*?" I asked her.

"Haha, *what*?" Erin went bright red. "Um. I mean maybe. Why…"

"*Which* boy?" I studied her like a scientist would a specimen.

"Nick Brooker," she replied.

"Oh, that's fine," I said. "He's OK I guess. He asked me out once. Obviously."

"Why *obviously*?" asked Erin. (As if *that* needed explanation!)

"OK Erin," I replied. "Well, I could sit here and say I'm worried my hair is too fluffy, or my nose is too big, but at the end of the day, we both know I read as *attractive* and everyone thinks I'm a snack."

Erin spluttered vaguely incredulous laughter, which I think was meant to suggest she thought I was arrogant, but I didn't care because #practisingselflove anyway.

Then she said, "Well, maybe he doesn't care about

*that*." (So she basically agreed that I am super hot. Ha.) "You know, he liked a picture of me in a zebra onesie," she went on, "so maybe he's not..." She trailed off.

"Did you want to use the word *superficial*?" I asked a tiny bit condescendingly.

"Um..."

"Because if you truly believed that; then what's with all this?" I waved a hand, gesturing to her face. "Finally mastering mascara etc.?"

Erin looked down, like she was thinking. Then she looked up again. "Did you go out with him? After he asked you out? Did you go out with him?"

"Oh! No." I shook my head.

"Why?"

"Not my type."

"What's wrong with him?"

"I don't know. Probably something. But there was just no *spark*. I'm sure he's nice though. He never lunged at me or anything."

"That seems like a low bar," said Erin. "No known assaults."

"Fine," I said magnanimously, forcing myself to be the grown-up. "Do you have the hots for him?"

"Maybe."

"Best of luck with your endeavours. Shall we get back to work now?"

"OK. But just one more…"

Erin tried to take a selfie of the two of us sitting at my mahogany dining table, working. She had to hold the phone far away to get us both in, and she dropped it on the marble chequerboard stone floor, and the screen cracked.

"Oh nooooo," she wailed. "It's cracked!"

What a fuss. Honestly. Was it not enough I'd gone out on a limb for her and risked alienating my friends? Not to mention inadvertently lowering my own social standing.

"Whatever," I sighed tiredly. "Just get your father to buy you a new one."

"*What?*" Erin looked at me shocked.

"You heard." I looked up perplexed. "Let's move on."

"OK, problem one: he can't afford to," said Erin.

"Well whatever, get it on the insurance."

"What insurance?"

"OK, *whatever*, you're from the mean streets," I replied tiredly. "Brilliant. You're an *outlaw*. You don't have phone insurance. *You're so cool.* But look, this is why we have rules and regulations. To protect us from our own stupidity."

"Ouch," said Erin, subdued. Then, "OK. I didn't realise how much I was annoying you. I'll go."

### ERIN

What the hell is *her* problem? I fumed, confused, all the bus ride home. I looked at the pictures I'd taken on my poor, cracked phone. I felt like I looked quite good in one of them, but I didn't have the heart to post any now. My mood had gone sour on the whole thing.

And I was annoyed, *too,* because something Grace had said had struck a chord. Why *was* I suddenly trying to look extra nice, if I really believed he liked me as I was? I had insecurities coming out the wazoo.

Nicole and I *officially* laugh at people who worry about stupid things like if their ears are too big. And here I am *trying to look pretty for a boy.* How unimaginative.

And why did Grace seem so irritable about selfies? She's normally all over selfies. That's what she *lives* for.

I calmed down a bit later when I got home.

I still can't work out if I'm a hypocrite for suddenly caring more about makeup. Google tells me that eyebrows take 56 days to grow back, which is basically two months. So, I guess if I'm still into it then, I'll know if I've become that which I once mocked.

# CHAPTER TWENTY-ONE

**Wednesday 20th March**

*GRACE*

Another brilliant poem by Grace Abella:

**Evergreen**
*The leaves are turning, turning brown*
*But not the evergreen*
*Look how they go red, look how they fall down,*
*What a thing to have seen.*

*They're pretty at first, then soon turn to slush*
*But not the evergreen*
*They're in people's way, when push comes to shove,*
*The ground won't look so clean.*

*The evergreen alone stands tall,*
*And keeps its pines aloft*
*Trusted, constant, reliable,*
*Through rain and sludge and frost.*

*When chaos rules, and wisdom sails,*
*The world is fickle, changing, mean,*
*The realm of nature may repeat its fails*
*But the evergreen is Queen.*

#naileditagain #whataminotgoodat

Actually, apologies. Well, let me rephrase that: on the *rare* occasions where I *have* actually made a mistake or done something wrong, I am very good at apologising. I believe in the rule of law and civilisation after all.

It's boring and laborious and I resent having to do it, but also I accept that it's the human condition and it just proves what a great person I am, that I am prepared to make the ultimate sacrifice and text Erin, "Sorry if I came off a bit abrupt before. Got a lot on my mind. Hope you can fix your phone."

So selfless. So kind.

Also, I really wanted to just get a tiny bit more work done on my story and I thought she'd never agree to come all the way to my house if I didn't acknowledge we'd had some kind of incident.

*You,* my diary, know that I am *not sorry at all,* and just playing her like a fiddle to get my own way.

Erin, though her faults are *many,* respects civilisation enough to comply with social norms and sent back, "Thx, nw. Let me know if U want 2 talk about anything."

Ha. No thank you. Abellas don't *talk* about our problems. We quit whining and get on with it.

I just wish she could hurry up with returning the RSVPs for her friends Nicole and Liz.

Maybe I should just chase them up myself?

#ifajobisworthdoing #superwomanbabes

### Thursday 21ˢᵗ March

*ERIN*

Ohhhhh maaaaaaaan.

Grace asked Nicole why she hadn't responded to the party invitation.

Nic honestly thought she was joking and that I

would never have forgotten to pass it on.

Ninety per cent sure Nic didn't buy the whole, *I've-been-so-busy-lately-I-really-did-forget-and-meant-to-invite-you-honestly-and-I'm-so-thrilled-you're-coming* excuse. I wouldn't buy it if it was the other way round to be fair.

Liz and Nic are now coming. We are hanging by a thread.

It's all such a shame because apart from my simmering resentment, Nic and I were actually getting on quite well. I was really pumped about Nick Brooker, and Nic *was* giving me really good advice.

Now I'm the terrible friend who gave her two days' notice to the hottest party in town.

# CHAPTER TWENTY-TWO

**Sunday 24<sup>th</sup> March**

*GRACE*

I am mostly a genius at parties. I chose *very* good caterers. Some of my friends are sophisticated enough to enjoy dim sum, and the rest enjoyed the miniature pizzas and tiny, tiny hamburgers. It was a nice touch having actual waiting staff.

Also, having adults around in some form helped keep some of the more boisterous revellers from getting too carried away and trashing anything.

I was very happy with the DJ and the lighting system, while the smoke machine added a certain *je ne sais quoi*.

Ditto the piñata – looked FAB! As did my ice

sculpture of a swan. And (as far as I know) only two boys got their tongues stuck on it this time.

I didn't manage to find a snow leopard, but maybe that was for the best.

I was really hoping that maybe my friends and Erin's friends would come together and see our worlds are not so different (not because I'm some damn hippy – just so I could be right and they could eat their words. Natch).

And, also, there would be no more mutinies and I would be top dog.

And, to be fair, everything went really well. To *start* with.

### ERIN

OK. First of all, it wasn't my fault!

Some of it might have been. But not all of it!

Nic was being kind of aggro to me from the start. (And YES I get why – and some of that *is* on me – but my patience and sympathy quickly waned.)

"Is that breakfast bar where you and *her majesty queen of swots* do your homework together?" she asked snarkily in the kitchen.

"Uh-huh." I tried to laugh it off and subtly look around for Nick Brooker, but I couldn't see him. "Hey! Let's have a go on the piñata!" I tried to change the subject, and Sophie Wheeler handed me the bat.

"Ugh, monobrow is here?" Theo said in my face, then walked past me. Nic smirked, which I found infuriating.

I watched him put way too much dip on a carrot stick. Then he ate it like a monster eating live rats. I thought how much I hated him. Urgh.

Sophie put the blindfold mask on my face.

"Make sure you make it tight," advised Nic. "We don't want any cheating."

I felt this weird shame creeping down my neck. But then it hit my stomach and fizzed into anger and started creeping back up again.

It was disorientating.

I mean, obviously – I couldn't see.

Plus, Sophie spun me round three times. I was dizzy and hot.

I felt chastised by Nic, and made a half-hearted attempt to hit the piñata. I know I wasn't even close. There was some muted giggling nearby.

"Come on mate, you're not *that* puny, are you?" Nic teased. Louder chuckles. I sensed people stopping to watch my embarrassment.

I regretted attempting to do the piñata at a cool party where I didn't really belong. I was making a spectacle of myself.

"Try and hit it," said a boy's voice. Chuckles.

"Come on monobrow!" jeered Theo.

I became more flustered and embarrassed. I had no idea which way the piñata even was now. The blindfold was really tight. Sophie had obeyed Nic's suggestion. I couldn't even see my feet out of the bottom to gauge which way the breakfast bar was.

I raised the bat up, as if getting ready to make a hit. This got more laughter. So did that mean it was the wrong way? I turned around. Less laughter. Was that better?

"Come on already, swotface!" Nic's voice. Laughter.

I was making a spectacle of myself. And Nicole, my best friend, was helping to spectacle me. I was betrayed and humiliated.

"Come on monobrow!"

I tried a hefty whack. I hit nothing. *More laughter*. I turned around and tried again. I could feel anger rising inside me.

"Come on monobrow!"

"Haaaa! Are you filming this?" Nic's voice. "Come on, swot!"

My humiliation finally boiled over into proper rage. I shouted, "STOP CALLING ME NAMES!" at the exact same time I gave a super hard whack. And hit something, *hard*. But it wasn't the piñata.

It all happened really fast. There was a clunk. A boy shouted, "Aaarrrgh!" Then came the noise of someone falling on expensive kitchen tiles, followed by the gasping of the crowd.

That all happened in a split second. Then time started again. Someone said, "Are you getting all this?" Someone else laughed.

I ripped off the blindfold. Two mobile phones were in my face, filming me. Theo was kneeling on the floor clutching his elbow in apparent agony. I had hit his arm.

"She could see!" shouted someone. "She hit Theo on purpose! Because he called her monobrow. She's a *psycho*!"

"No, I didn't!" I cried. "Stop filming me! It was an accident!"

Theo looked close to tears. Maybe he was just in shock. "She's a psycho!" he yelled. Then he got up and ran away.

I'm pretty sure he ran away because he was embarrassed and didn't want anyone to see him crying.

"Oh my god," people were muttering. The phones were put down though. No one was filming me any more. But a crowd was gathering, and so were whispers that I had tried to kill Theo in vengeance.

"People! People! Stop!" Nicole shouted over the hubbub, and got relative silence (the music was in the room next door). "Are you kidding yourselves? Look at who you're talking about!"

Everyone looked me up and down and then back to Nic. "Seriously, look at her!" They glanced at me again. "Erin doesn't have a psycho bone in her body! She's the *nerdiest*, quietest little swot and she wouldn't hurt a fly!"

"STOP CALLING ME A SWOT!" I heard myself shout. "STOP IT! JUST STOP IT! I'm *not* a swot!

I'm just a normal person! I hate when you call me swot! It makes me feel really bad and guilty, like I've done something wrong, and I haven't! It's not *my* fault I got moved up two sets in English! I would never ever, *ever* call you stupid! I never call you anything mean! Stop calling me swot!"

The angry words just bubbled out of me.

Nic's eyes filled with tears. "I was defending you!" she whispered, looking stricken.

"Great!" I shouted sarcastically. "Well, with friends like you, who needs enemies!"

Nic stared at me, incredulous, and then her heartbroken eyes kind of hardened and glazed over. "You ARE a psycho!" she spat, then she and Liz turned and ran off too.

It was at this point that Brianna and Sylvie arrived on the scene, dragging Grace with them. "Here!" said Brianna.

"She's here," agreed Sylvie.

Oh phew, Grace was here. She was my friend. Some cavalry, a friendly face. *She sticks up for me now*, I thought. I was sure she could sort all this out and tell everyone it was an accident and that I'm not a psycho.

"Did you – ?" Grace blinked at me quizzically. "Did you really hit Theo with the piñata bat?"

"Yes!" snapped Sylvie.

"It was an accident," I said in a small voice.

"Look at the video!" Brianna held up her phone.

"Oh my god, is that already on Instagram?" I said.

"Yes, it is, *psycho*," said Brianna.

"And Snapchat," said Chloe, joining them from the crowd.

"You have to chuck her out," added Sylvie. "It's not safe for her to be here. She assaulted one of your guests. Who knows what she's capable of."

"It was an accident," I repeated.

"We can't take that risk," stated Brianna. She turned to address Grace. "*Babes*, she's destroyed the whole vibe of your party. No one wants her here."

Grace looked to each person's face, then back to me. "All right, Erin, come with me." She reached for my hand and then let it drop as I followed her out into the hallway.

She led me towards her front door. OMG she *was* chucking me out! Surely not! She was supposed to be my friend! She knew I would never do anything psychotic. *Surely*.

"You're not *actually* chucking me out, are you?" I asked, loitering pointlessly by her antique hat stand.

"It's nothing personal," she replied. "I'm *trying* to have a nice party. Maybe it's better you leave, let the dust settle?"

"But it was an accident! Don't you believe me?"

"Well, *yeah*. I mean, I certainly wouldn't have *thought* you'd be the type of person to hit someone with a bat *on purpose*." She paused. "But you know, I think you're maybe going through some things with your friend Nicole and I don't know … maybe it would do you good to get some fresh air and calm down and stuff."

"Wow," I said. "I thought you were my friend."

"I am your friend."

"Why didn't you stick up for me then?"

"Look, *I* could say I feel let down by *you*," replied Grace haughtily. "I went out on a *limb* for you. I've really tried to include you in my friendship group. I can't single-handedly heal the ills wreaked by the *laws of the playground*. All *you* had to do was act normal for two seconds, and apparently that was too much to ask. So here we are."

"*Unbelievable*," I said. "You are a total coward,

you know that? If you don't like me, fine. But don't pretend you have principles."

"I think you're going through something hard right now," said Grace. "Look, if it's any consolation I forgive you for disrupting my party by hitting someone. No ill feelings."

"Wow. That's a big consolation, yes, thanks. I feel much better." I said this sarcastically but I'm not sure the sarcasm registered with Grace.

"Good. So, you see, we can still be friends. In fact," Grace seemed to switch mode to admin, "when is the deadline for the ghost story again?"

"*Really?*" I was flabbergasted (and still sarcastic). "You think that's an appropriate question to ask me right now?" She nodded. "Well, that's just great!" I fumed. "It's –"

Huh. I paused. Was *I* about to try to teach *Grace* a lesson? Take back a tiny modicum of control on the worst day of my life? "It's the first of April," I responded.

"April Fools?" said Grace.

"Yep. Bye forever Grace." I left, under a cloud of shame, to enter the new friendless, betrayed phase of my existence.

"See you soon!" she called after me.

She genuinely seemed to have no idea I was upset with her. And certainly no idea that the ghost story competition deadline was *not* the 1<sup>st</sup> of April, but the 28<sup>th</sup> of March.

# CHAPTER TWENTY-THREE

***GRACE***

It was a long Sunday for some reason. Even though Daddy took us to an *exquisite* gastro pub. I had this gnawing feeling about Erin. Like, maybe I hadn't been completely … *fair* to her.

And I tried to tell myself that if anything *I* should be annoyed *with her*. Because she nearly ruined my party … but … but (a) every party needs a good *story*, and her hitting Theo sort of was that; and (b) I *know* she didn't do it on purpose. And *actually*, (c) Theo is a little creep who sort of deserved it anyway.

Something Erin said has really stayed with me: *coward*.

Abellas are not cowards!

But *did* I pander to my friends instead of doing the *less popular* but right thing?

Because, actually, what is the *point* of being popular if you can't control everyone and be a highly influential style icon all the time? And if I'm not that, then what even *am* I?

I'd been really torturing myself about why my group of friends aren't hanging off my every word. And what that says about me, and about them. And the paradox is if they won't listen to me, they must be idiots, but if they *are* idiots, I should be able to outsmart them and make them listen to me … and aaarrrggghhh.

Maybe I let that worry cloud my judgement?

I tried to turn my brain off and enjoy the fact that *most* of my party *had* been a success. And I had behaved honourably and impeccably throughout. But I was still thinking about Erin when I got into bed!

I needed comfort, so I snuggled up with *Jane Eyre* and read for a bit.

I've re-read that book so many times that sometimes I just pick it up and start reading at random, for comfort.

I ended up reading the bit towards the end, about how Jane Eyre becomes great friends with her new cousins.

Hadn't I become great friends with Erin? Maybe I really *had* treated her badly. That was why I felt bad.

I, Grace Abella, had behaved badly.

Abellas don't make a habit of mistakes, but when we do, we admit them.

I will apologise to Erin.

I REALLY shouldn't have put my other friends' wishes above what I knew was right. Poor Erin.

And like, I love my friends and everything. #lovemygirlsquad. But sometimes, *sometimes* that whole world is just *exhausting*. It's a constant effort to stay on high alert and put people down if they start dissing you.

But it was nice to hang out with Erin and not worry about any of those status games. There was no constant pressure to be cool or on guard for slights.

And who cares what my other friends think? They'll come around eventually. They always do. No one believed me about the lob haircut and then *that* was very on trend, and everyone had to eat their words.

So what if I disagree with them for a bit? I'll just be a different type of style icon or whatever. Maybe I'm entering my alternative phase…

I wonder if I should do something to make things up with Erin? Like maybe I need to apologise *for real* – not my fake smoothing things over kind. And maybe get her a present? As a good-will gesture to show her I'm serious?

Hmmm, what does Erin need? A phone! (I can't get her a new phone – that's way too over the top.) Something smaller … a cupcake! OK, that's probably too small. I was more horrible than a cupcake. I need something somewhere between those two things…

# CHAPTER TWENTY-FOUR

**Monday 25th March**

*ERIN*

Fun new discovery: when one is sent to Coventry in disgrace, one no longer gets called names all day long.

Tiny YAY.

Nic and Liz ignored and whispered about me in the form room before registration.

No eye contact from any of my peers.

I think maybe people are *scared* of me?

Not going to lie, this is the closest I've ever been to high status, and part of me likes it. I mean, it is, in *some* ways, an improvement.

Theo waltzed into the form room this morning,

clocked me, jumped, turned around and took a wide berth round the desks to avoid me.

I am very happy to let him continue to think I hit him on purpose.

That's right, Theo, keep away – you drove me to breaking point and now I could *flip out* again at any time.

I sat down at my desk before morning registration. I ignored the whispers of Liz and Nic.

I was pretty shocked when Grace marched up to my desk, proffering what looked like a present.

"What do you want?" I half whispered, shocked.

Nic and Liz were straining to listen but pretending not to be.

"Erin, I should very much like to apologise to you." Grace managed to somehow sound dignified.

I felt bizarrely awkward.

"Go away," I hissed.

"I really would like to most sincerely apologise," Grace repeated. "I should have supported you at my party more. I know you didn't hit Theo on purpose. I never should have thrown you out. I have got you this present to show you how sorry I am."

"Holy *what*?" Nic blurted out. "You chucked her out of your party? Great new best friend you have here." She addressed me.

Grace held out a red sparkly gift bag. Inside was a sleek, silver-looking makeup bag and some quite fancy makeup.

"Wait. Is that *Dior*?" asked Liz.

"Yes, I find I really like their mascara," said Grace. "And Erin is not my best friend, she's yours." Grace addressed Nic.

"Can I have a *look*?" Liz reached for the bag and I handed it to her.

"*Huh*," scoffed Nic. "No, you won her fair and square. I can't keep up with all the intellectual Brontë crap and marble kitchens and *Dior* makeup. You keep her. Now maybe get lost, yeah?"

Grace did not like being spoken to like that. She raised an eyebrow haughtily.

"There's a lot of pain in you *babe*."

"Is *that* what this is about?" I asked Nic. "You thought you couldn't keep up with *me*?"

"Of course," Grace answered for Nic. "Nicole is very insecure about her intelligence. I think that's why she lashes out, and probably why she places so much emphasis on the importance of music, to deflect."

"You *what*?" Nic stood up.

"You heard," Grace replied evenly.

"You patronising *cow*!" spat Nic. "You don't know anything about me!" She grabbed the bag of makeup from Liz. "Take your crap and get lost!"

Nic forcefully shoved the bag back towards Grace, and sort of pushed her a tiny bit at the same time.

"*Hey!*" That was Sylvie from across the room.

Then Sylvie, Brianna and Chloe all strutted over to us.

"Do we have a problem here?" asked Sylvie menacingly.

"No," said Grace evenly. She rolled her eyes.

"Oh, *really*?" said Brianna, staring daggers at Nicole.

"It looks like some basic skank is giving you side eye," said Sylvie.

"Babes, I got this," said Grace. She was really calm. I was filling with adrenaline at all the unwanted drama.

"Well, just so you know," Sylvie addressed Nicole and me, but mainly Nicole, "the last time some *skank*

 tried to push one of us, she ended up falling down some stairs."

Brianna chuckled, then she and Sylvie did a weirdly cool hi-five without actually looking at each other. Then they held hands for a second, before dropping their hands back down and continuing to stare me and Nic down.

"Well, the last time someone called me a *skank*, she got her teeth knocked down her throat," said Nicole (quite bravely, I thought).

"Yawn," said Grace, sounding bored. "You all done being *extra*?"

"Babes, you can't let these emo witches *step* to you. Even if one of them is *psycho*." Sylvie glared at me.

"All right, you know what? You all need to hear this," said Grace. "Erin is *not* psycho. She's my friend. She's funny and kind and she would never do that on purpose. *Sure*, she doesn't have *great* fashion sense," Brianna and Sylvie nodded emphatically at this, "but it would be *boring* if we were all the same." Grace continued, "I never should have chucked her out of my party and I'm sorry, Erin. I want to be friends. So, if anyone is disrespectful to Erin you will

194

have a problem with me." She paused. "And Nicole, I don't know what you've got going on with Erin, but I hope you become friends again because Erin is great and you're lucky to have her." Nicole was about to retort, but Grace continued, "Erin, please take this as a token of how sorry I am," and passed the bag back to me.

I took it numbly. "Um, OK…" I mumbled.

"Sylvie, Brianna, Chloe, apologise to Erin," Grace instructed.

"*What?!* Chloe didn't even do anything," protested Sylvie.

"I'm sorry Erin," said Chloe dutifully.

"*Eurgh*, fine." Brianna rolled her eyes. "Sorry, Erin."

"Sorry, Erin," said Sylvie.

"Great. See you later Erin." Grace beamed at me and they left.

"Well, you may have *them* twisted round your little finger," said Nic then. "But I'm not buying it."

"Buying *what*?" I asked her, confused.

"You really hurt my feelings at that party. I'm still really upset with you. And you haven't even apologised to me."

"OK, I'm sorry I upset you, but do you know why? *I'm upset with you too*, I have trouble telling you sometimes how—"

"*Not interested*," Nic cut me off. "Is that your idea of an apology? Because I can't even." She did a sassy hand gesture to me. My two separate groups of friends were more similar than I had realised.

"Nic, you should listen to my side," I attempted.

"No," Nic snapped. "You don't even care about *my side*. I think you need to have a long, hard think about how much you've upset me actually. I'm not talking to you. I seriously can't even."

She turned her chair away and sat down so she was facing Liz.

"Nic I'm just trying to be –" *Honest*. I didn't finish my sentence.

I'm just trying to be honest.

Just like how I need to tell Grace that I lied to her about the competition deadline.

Ohhhhhhh sugar.

### GRACE

I *knew* I could fix it! I knew I could fix it if I could just put my head together, with my other head. (My head is so brilliant it counts as most people's two heads. I am a genius.) #sowhatelseisnew

Well, everything. This is it. New me. New everything. I am going to be a *new person*. A more authentic person… Like maybe everything doesn't have to look *perfect* on Instagram. And in other ways… I'll get there.

But the main point is: Erin is still my friend and I fixed it and that is awesome.


### *ERIN*

OK, it's 9pm and I *still* haven't told Grace the real deadline for the ghost story competition. *Why haven't I told her?*

It would be so easy … just text, call her, email her! TELL HER AT SCHOOL.

She looked *so pleased* when she thought I still wanted her to be my friend. She'll never look at me that way again if I tell her. (Maybe she'll never find out…?) Oh, she so will…

As soon as she emails it in late and gets an email bounce back that she's missed the deadline. Or if she even uses Google herself…?

I could say it was a mistake…? But I don't make

mistakes like that.

Aaaaarrrgghhh.

And what a weird day! So much drama! And I was at the centre of it for some reason. Maybe Grace just attracts drama wherever she goes, and so now some has rubbed off on me?

And now I'm sitting here in bed, writing this diary, feeling *terrible*. I'm torn and don't know what to do.

*Why haven't I told her?* I can't believe I didn't just tell her straight away. Is it too late to come forward already? Maybe I could explain it all tomorrow somehow.

Am I still *annoyed*?

OMG am I? Is that why I haven't come forward? I still secretly want to *punish* Grace even though she already seems to have seen the error of her ways? *And* I *do* want to be friends with her – so badly that I will even risk not telling her in case she doesn't like me any more after. (WHAT?!)

THAT MAKES NO SENSE. WHY IS THIS SO COMPLICATED? Why are my feelings so complicated? What is wrong with me?

Kiera said – when I told her – that I'm ridiculous. She took *great pleasure* in reminding me that just the other day I was worried I didn't have any *real friends*, and now here we are; I have one friend publicly declaring their love for me and the other so hurt by the loss of my friendship that she can't think straight.

I told Kiera she was mad.

And that Nic really seems to hate me, actually. She was kind of venomous.

But Kiera thinks that Nic is just really hurt and insecure and has a massive ego. She reckons she couldn't handle my rise in intelligence status and felt threatened, and so had to put me down to compensate.

Which is all very well as an explanation, but how are you supposed to explain to an insecure person with a sensitive ego that they have actually hurt *your* feelings quite a lot too?

OK. I should definitely tell Grace the truth. It's the right thing to do. I'll definitely tell her. Tomorrow. Definitely.

I've GOT to start being more honest and telling people things they don't want to hear sooner. Before it escalates. Like it did with Nic.

# CHAPTER TWENTY-FIVE

**Wednesday 27ˢᵗ March**

***GRACE***
EMAIL
19.56
FROM: GRACE ABELLA
TO: CHARLOTTE BRONTË FAN CLUB
SUBJECT: RE: GHOST STORY

Dear Mrs Wilson and Erin,
Take two! Ahead of schedule (as ever!) I've made the changes that Erin suggested, about carbolic soap and everything. I think Erin's feedback was really helpful and I've enjoyed working on this together! Hope you found my notes as useful, Erin! Can't wait

to read yours.

Best,

Grace

## The Secret Room

*By Grace Abella*

Everyone had always assumed that Mary Miller was a good girl. She had all the characteristics that would indicate this was the case. Mary was shy and polite, and, if anything, a little diffident. She was well-turned out and always washed herself with carbolic soap.

Mary worked in the factory and brought home her wages to her father and did as she was told. She cooked the meals and kept the house and looked after the chickens and the dog. The house was neat and had a decorative plate on the wall that said, "Long Live Queen Victoria".

No one would have suspected her of *anything*.

Sarah Juniper was a *different* story. She was loud, opinionated and sometimes swore. She had lived alone with her cat in her cottage in the woods ever since her father had died. No one had ever liked or trusted her.

There were occasional whispers that some believed her to be a witch. But she was an excellent seamstress and so she continued to be given work in the village, despite her unpopularity.

Mary and Sarah became acquaintances at the factory. Mary helped to make the fabric that Sarah would go on to sew. They soon started spending more time together, unlikely though the pairing was. The villagers just hoped that Mary would be a good influence on Sarah.

When the first child went missing, there was a huge hunt, and everyone went looking. Nothing was found, not even a body, and everyone feared that wolves or bears must be responsible.

When the second child went missing, a chill set in over the village and everyone became very afraid. Children were ordered to stay in groups of three or more.

At the third missing child, the sense of dread hung like a cloud over them. A curfew was introduced, and men from the village started patrolling in vigilante shifts, in order to try and protect those remaining.

And then the whispers started. And the whispers

turned into a murmur, and the murmur turned into a hubbub, and the hubbub turned into a *ROAR* that Sarah Juniper must be responsible – SHE MUST BE A WITCH.

And so they marched on Sarah Juniper's cottage in the woods. And they found a *locked room* with four beds containing the three children, asleep but alive.

Sarah seemed to be in a funny state where she couldn't remember things. She claimed she was trying to help *save* the children, but she wasn't able to explain from whom.

So the villagers hanged Sarah from the tree outside her own cottage on suspicion of being a witch and of kidnapping children.

The children were brought home but could not be woken up. A call went out to find a physician from another village that could help. The men stopped patrolling the village and instead went hunting for assistance.

If they could just get these sleeping children to wake up, everything could go back to normal. The witch was *dead* after all. It was all going to be fine now.

AND THEN

A *fourth* child went missing.

AND THEN

The *first three* children disappeared again.

The villagers searched Sarah Juniper's cottage from top to bottom and the surrounding area, but to no avail.

*No one* thought to look in Mary Miller's house. No one thought to look in her attic where she kept her spell book and four beds with four sleeping children in them.

And no one noticed as the years went by that Mary Miller didn't age.

Until one day, twenty years later, on the anniversary of Sarah Juniper's hanging, there was a fire.

No one knew how it could have started, but it looked like a candle had somehow fallen on to a giant book in the attic. One person said they saw a cat leaping out of a small attic window, moments before the blaze took hold.

When the villagers put out the fire, they found four sleeping children – unharmed and un-aged in the attic – and the burnt body of an elderly woman who looked a bit like Mary Miller.

Legend has it that once a year, on the anniversary

of her death, the ghost of Sarah Juniper can be seen walking through the village, noose still around her neck, holding her cat.

***ERIN***

Oh god. Oh god. I haven't told her.

Escalation.

Ohhhh suuuuggggar.

Why haven't I told her? I've had SO many opportunities in the last two days… What's wrong with me?! Oh nooooo! Mrs Wilson has replied! My lies are about to come crashing down around me.

Why haven't I told her???

EMAIL
20.21
FROM: MRS WILSON
TO: CHARLOTTE BRONTË FAN CLUB
SUBJECT: GHOST STORY

Dear Grace and Erin,

I don't think that's quite right. I had the deadline as Thursday 28th – tomorrow – so you're only just in time! Better hand it in soon. I'm sure the changes you've

made are great!

Erin – you'd better hand yours in too!

Best,

**Mrs Wilson**

*Second in Department for English*

## *GRACE*

Oh dear. How embarrassing for her. And odd. Erin is usually quite good at these things, but she has told both of us the wrong date – wait, *what*?

## *ERIN*

EMAIL

20.26

FROM: MRS WILSON

TO: CHARLOTTE BRONTË FAN CLUB

SUBJECT: GHOST STORY

Dear Mrs Wilson and Grace,

I actually handed mine into the competition already. I did it on Sunday evening. I didn't want to hand it in for feedback on Sunday because, well, I just wasn't feeling very well. So I just thought I'd quickly do it and get it over with. I'm sorry for any confusion.

Best,

Erin

## *GRACE*

OMG! That little *snake*! She did this on *purpose*! She tried to *sabotage* my *whole career* as a *writer*! I can't believe it! (Or maybe I can?) But I don't want to… *I can't believe it*!!!

OMG, I was *right* all along. Erin is a terrible person, made by the devil to torment me!

It *can't* have been an accident. Or a coincidence. It just can't.

I feel like such a fool. I made myself *vulnerable* (for possibly the first time ever). I told everyone to be nice to her! I publicly declared that she was great!

I *trusted* her. Against my own brain's better judgement. I thought I'd had some kind of *breakthrough* and become a nicer, better person … but no.

I was *right* when I thought she was evil, stealing my favourite teacher and my career.

I'm not sure I've ever been this angry and this sad before.

# CHAPTER TWENTY-SIX

**Thursday 28th March**

*ERIN*

I (admittedly belatedly) thought I should try and face the music head on.

I went up to Grace in the form room, first thing. "Hi Grace, I think I should explain—"

"Oh! Ew!" Grace waved her hand in front of her nose dramatically, like she could smell something terrible. A few people turned to watch her. "What is that *smell*?"

Sylvie and Brianna were already amused in anticipation.

"It smells like *sewers*!" Grace wrinkled up her nose. "Mixed with *halitosis*!"

*Hey, that's one of the words from my word list!* I thought, ridiculously.

Also, no one else really knew what halitosis meant, so that got less of a laugh than the *sewers* bit from Grace's audience.

Sylvie and Brianna decided to join in – maybe they were worried Grace was losing her touch by using unknown words. Ironic that me, the one person who knew and enjoyed the word halitosis, was also the victim of its use. (Did that sum up our whole relationship?)

"It smells like someone barfed up a dead animal!" gloated Sylvie. (Laughter.)

"Mixed with plague-ridden fish guts!" added Brianna gleefully. (Laughter.)

"And then mixed with… a portaloo … on day four of Glastonbury!" (Only chuckles.)

This was Chloe's offering. *Too specific Chloe, slowing it down*, I thought silently. They frowned at her slightly.

"Sorry. Were you saying something? So difficult to concentrate because of the *stench*." Grace finally addressed me, still flapping her hand, but slower.

"OK. Well, I think you've answered my question,"

209

I replied. "I was going to try and explain. But cool to know where I stand." I turned, red-faced and walked back to my desk.

"See you later Elmo!" Grace called after me, to much laughter from her friends.

Nic and Liz stopped whispering long enough for Nic to look up at me and smirk as I came over to my desk.

"Uh-oh, trouble in paradise?" said Nic.

"Please leave me alone," I said quietly, feeling very dejected and hot.

"Seen through all your lies, have they? That's a shame," she gloated. "Bad times for little swotty swot face."

"I don't like it when you call me swot," I said calmly and evenly.

"Well, I don't like it when you –" Nic paused. Odd. I looked up at her. Couldn't she think of something?

"You don't like it when I what?" I asked her. "*Have other friends?*"

Nic looked troubled, like she was genuinely grappling with a conundrum.

"Not any more, you don't," she quipped. And then she went back to whispering to Liz.

## GRACE

Oh, it is ON. Like Donkey Kong. Or something cooler. (I'll think of much cooler stuff again once I've got Erin out of my head.)

You want to do this with me? It's *go time*.

"*Ooops*." I knocked Erin's hand when she was writing in English and made a huge line across her page. Brianna and Sylvie convulsed in silent giggles.

"*And that's how we do that*," I whispered in Erin's ear.

"Don't cry," whispered Sylvie. "You're not going to cry, are you?"

Erin was red-faced, but she still looked me right in the eye. "I'm sorry," she whispered. "You haven't let me explain." She looked a bit sad. Then she set about trying to fix the mess I'd made of her writing.

"Did you *really* think you could get away with it?" I whispered to her then. "Did you really think someone like *you* could try and trick me and *win*?"

"I really wasn't trying to do that," Erin whispered back. "I let *you* explain to *me*… *Before*."

Some scrunched up paper hit Erin on the forehead.

It was a good aim by Brianna. Subtle too, as Mrs Wilson didn't notice. "Don't cry!" whispered Brianna, triumphantly.

I didn't feel guilty. I *don't* feel guilty! I mean, look how sneaky she was!

She *secretly* re-wrote her story (with all of the useful and brilliant notes I gave her) and then *secretly* handed it in!

She made a *conscious choice* to do that, deliberately not putting it under my nose. So as not to arouse my competitive streak and make me want to hand mine in early too!

She didn't want to draw attention to her crime! *So underhanded*. She *wanted* me to fail! *That's so hurtful*.

*(Also, it was the Sunday after I chucked her out of my party and she might not have been thinking straight and wanted revenge and – shut up brain!)*

She is not justified in doing what she did. And she could have told me *since* then.

"*Don't cry,*" smirked Sylvie.

"I've said sorry," whispered Erin, mainly to me, but so that they could all hear it. "Anything you do now *isn't* whatever your idea of punishing me is. It's actually *bullying*."

"Oooooh," whispered Sylvie in a high-pitched voice.

"Big word for little Elmo," whispered Brianna.

"Three whole syllables," commented Sylvie.

I privately marvelled at how assertive Erin was being. When she first arrived in our group, she could barely make eye-contact with any of us. Now she was attempting to stand her ground and defend herself. And she was outnumbered.

It was almost impressive. Or it would be if she wasn't such a sneaky snake. (Ha, alliteration – I'm a genius.)

I expect that *actually*, since Erin had been exposed to my good manners and the enigmatic way in which I comport myself, she probably couldn't help but take notes and copy my confidence. Well, guess what? You've stolen my energy for the last time, weasel face.

"*Don't cry*," I whispered to her coldly. And the others laughed.

# CHAPTER TWENTY-SEVEN

**Friday 29th March**

*ERIN*

I don't know why I'm disappointed or why I thought anything would be any different.

*Of course* they are bullying me worse than ever before. *Of course* English is now a living nightmare. *Of course* I have gained and then lost a new friend at rapid speed.

But I guess at least I had two more days of being Grace's friend before she found out I'd lied. If I'd told her straight away, and this was how she'd reacted, I'd have had two extra horrible days...

Or maybe she'd have forgiven me?

*Why am I so bad at telling people things I think*

*they don't want to hear?*

I know I should rip more band aids off and face my fear and everything. But also, every time I tried that with Nic, she wouldn't listen.

I don't think *all* of this is my fault. I mean, I'm definitely *at fault*, for sure. But it's not *completely* my fault. Doesn't really make much difference though. The result is I have no friends and am all alone. Which was sort of my worst fear to begin with, diary.

Trying to keep friends by not telling them when they upset you – or when you have sort of lied to them because they chucked you out of a party – backfires and you lose them anyway.

If I had managed to tell Nic I didn't like some of the stuff she said sooner, maybe it wouldn't have all burbled out of me in a moment of crisis and we *could* have talked about it? I don't know.

Nic's being weird with me, actually. I mean, obviously, she's not speaking to me, fine. But it's like there's less menace behind it now. And every now and then I catch her looking at me, almost wistfully. Like maybe she misses me? I don't know. It could all just be in my head.

I thought it best to give Grace back the makeup

present she gave me. It seemed like an expensive gift and wrong for me to hold on to it, now that we're not friends any more. And I hadn't used any of it yet because I felt guilty. I couldn't face any more confrontations, so I just left it on her desk with a note for her to find at the end of lunch.

One day I *will* get better at confrontations. But not today.

Back to the drawing board. Another Friday night *in*, where I sit and contemplate everything I've done wrong and try and do homework. Woo.

Never try to do new things or let anyone in, appears to be the lesson here. Though *not* according to Kiera.

She got sick of me sighing while lying down on the lower bunk, while she was sitting at our "desk" (small plank of wood attached to the wall) colouring in some maps for her geography homework. I wasn't even sighing *that* dramatically. So I don't know why she thought that.

"And the Oscar for most dramatic sigh while lying in a bunk bed goes to…!" Kiera did a drum roll on the plank/desk.

"I'm not—"

"Eriiin Browwwwn!" Kiera interrupted.

"In the mood," I finished.

"Woo! Go Erin!" Kiera continued anyway. "Who would you like to thank? Besides baby Jesus?"

"Shut up," I said tiredly.

"What's that? Your *sister*? For being such a great inspiration, and for putting up with all your ridiculous mood swings? That's so sweet, thanks!"

I couldn't help but laugh at that. "Very good," I muttered.

"Ha," said Kiera, pleased. Then, "You still sad about your new friend?"

"*Ex*-new friend," I reminded her. "And ex-*best* friend. The whole general absence of *any friends* thing." I had already updated Kiera with all the dejected details. (Ha, alliteration.)

"It sounds like she really likes you," said Kiera, going back to her colouring. "They both do."

"Then you're not listening, because she hates me," I said. "They both do."

"Of course they both still like you," said Kiera. "Who wouldn't like *you*? You're easy going and kind. Everyone wants to be friends with the gentle, easy going little poet soul of Erin Brown."

I couldn't help but giggle. "What are you even

talking about?" I asked her.

"You're not as easy going as *me*," stated Kiera. "But they don't see these mopey mood swings of yours."

"Ha, alliteration," I interjected.

"So, as well as annoying stuff like that," said Kiera, "sometimes you're a bit negative I suppose. But otherwise, solid friend material."

"I mean…" I tried to respond appropriately. "That's probably the nicest thing you've ever said to me."

"Sure. I'm nice too. We're conflict avoiders, because of our…" Kiera cupped her hands around her mouth to sing "…parents' divooooorce, oh yeah."

I really had to laugh. I just couldn't help it. And I have no idea how singing those words transformed the effect from *awful* to the funniest thing ever, but there you go. My sister is a genius. God, I love my sister.

"You *are* really nice," I told her. "And funny and easy going."

She nodded sagely. "I know. That's probably how we attract these highly strung people into our lives. They want to learn to chill."

"Is someone giving *you* grief?" I asked her.

"Nothing I can't handle," said Kiera. "The first rule of dance troupe is: Mia is *not* in charge of dance troupe. Any more. Everyone got sick of her excessive use of jazz hands in the end. I didn't even have to do anything."

"Oh, um, OK, cool."

"My point is," said Kiera, "it sounds like Nic is on the verge of initiating an apology sequence, and Grace is still just really hurting."

"You reckon?"

"Yes, definitely," responded Kiera. "She sounds like quite a prideful person who doesn't often let people in. That kind of person takes things like what you did *really badly*. I mean, look at Dad."

"What's it got to do with *Dad*?" I was bemused.

"Remember when Mum forgot to tell him that everyone was supposed to wear a Christmas jumper to our old neighbours' party, and he didn't wear one and got the nickname *Scroogey McScrooge Face*?"

"Yeah. Wow. Our old neighbours weren't the best at making up nicknames, were they?" I replied.

"No. Well that boat thing had just happened."

"Yeah. He thought she'd done that jumper thing on purpose and didn't speak to any of us, for like

a month. And they have since got, as you say…"
I sang "…*divoooorced*, so I don't see how your
point stands here."

"My point," Kiera pauses grandly, "is that Grace
didn't *have* to give you that expensive makeup. She
was trying to express love the only way she's been
shown…"

I laughed and Kiera giggled. "You're talking such
rubbish. And I have since given it back," I said.

"I still say she really likes you," said Kiera. "I think
you still have a shot. Like follow her to an airport or
something."

We both giggled again.

How am I *worse* at life than my eleven-year-old
sister? I guess she *is* nearly twelve.

### GRACE

I'd be lying if said I wasn't a *little* surprised that
the "sorry present" I gave Erin was returned to me
(stealthily – as is Erin's way, *natch*) and was waiting
on my desk at the end of lunch, along with a scrawled
note that said: "It seems wrong to keep this now.
Erin."

I mean, *honestly*. I suppose on one level, one *could*

interpret that as noble; but on another level – *rude*.

But no matter. Because things are BACK TO NORMAL.

I totally see why my friends had been so suspicious of Erin now. Obviously she was super weird and devious the whole time and I just couldn't see it.

Which is unlike me, but I guess that I am just so nice that sometimes people take advantage of it? Well, that doesn't really sound like me either.

I don't have an adequate explanation yet actually. There are a few contradictory things happening.

But I decided to try not to dwell on it too much because I was going out on Friday night! FRIDAY NIGHT BABY YEAH. Like the good old days.

I had LOADS of fun getting dressed up, *just like I always used to*. I took a mirror selfie, *just like I always used to*, showcasing my new silver earrings and super cute jacket. I posted it online, *just like I always used to*. "Rocking my new threads." #treatyourself #lovemylife #howistyle #ootd #thisgirlcan #fridaynightwoo

Actually, it wasn't *quite* as much fun as it used to be, as I felt a tiny bit self-conscious about taking so many attempts to get the perfect selfie. Like I could see Erin's bemused face, even if she wasn't there. And then I felt weirdly nostalgic for the theatre trip I took with Erin, when she first judged my selfie-taking.

And then I had to remind myself that Erin sucks and I don't like her.

No. I refuse to let Erin ruin my fun. She's gone from my life. So I scratch that from the record, diary. It was *just* as much fun as usual.

And actually, Erin was *all over* selfies these days anyway. So, if she *was* here, she wouldn't be looking at me with her judgey face, she'd be looking at me with her *impressed* face, but – ANYWAY – I'm not *thinking* about Erin. I'm *glad* she's not here.

Daddy's car dropped me off outside Byron Burger, where my friends were waiting, and we squealed and hugged each other *just like we always used to*. And it was *just* as much fun.

We took the obligatory selfies and we all looked smoking hot, and no one embarrassed themselves by saying *on fleek*.

I didn't ponder *for a moment* why it was weird how that's an offence to my group of friends. And how words are transient and change their meaning, and surely it's the *intent* behind them that's more important? And I *certainly* didn't think about how interesting it was that Erin made a word list, with words like halitosis and diffident on it.

Like I said, I *didn't* think that. I was having just as much fun as *usual*. I wasn't lachrymose.

We had *so much fun* in the restaurant. Sylvie had brought some fun party stuff because everyone wanted to celebrate that I am back to normal. (Which I might have been slightly offended by, if I stopped to think about it. So I didn't.) Fun fun fun.

So, she put these fun little gold letters and pictures of cakes all over the table (which was kind of messy but looked really good) and we all had party whistles that we could blow, which were great, and not "obnoxious" like I think I might have heard someone at the next table saying.

And a waiter had to tell us to keep it down a bit, and that the gold letters were making a mess. So Sylvie lied and said it was my birthday. And then the waiter had to bring me a little piece of cake and a party hat, and then the whole restaurant had to sing happy birthday to me! It was *wild*!

We got so many great photos of the gold letters

and everything. Some very arty shots. And everyone wanted a turn with the hat, even though it was ridiculous.

And we even got milkshakes afterwards.

Then we took a great photo of all of us drinking our milkshakes. Sylvie posted it with the caption, "Only ice-cold milkshakes can cool these hotties down! #youcantsitwithus #therealgirlsquad #fullonsnacks #milkshakebringsalltheboystotheyard #nofakers

And I reposted it, obviously. With the captions #lovemylife #lovemygirls #dreamteam

And then they all went to the loo but I stayed sitting at the table, and I accidentally contemplated whether I *did* love my life and my girls, and I wasn't quite sure.

All of my Instagram makes it look like I'm having the best time.

It was sort of weird how I wasn't enjoying my friends' company quite as much now that I was back in it for the long haul. *Long haul?* That sounds wrong. Like I was *trapped* or something! I didn't feel trapped. I was *happy*. Definitely. Everything was back to *normal*.

Except…

Except it was a bit like … when you are eating something and then you try another food and then you can't go back to the first food because it tastes weird after the other one…

Like, if you're eating yoghurt, and then you eat a satsuma, and then you go back to the yoghurt, and the yoghurt tastes weird, because your tongue is all acidic or whatever. Or how you basically can't eat anything after a pickled onion, for ages.

I'm not saying Erin was a pickled onion. I'm saying she was a satsuma. And my friends were yoghurts.

I realised I wasn't making complete sense in my own head. But also that I wasn't having as much fun as I had hoped.

And then I took a *serious* photo of myself, looking a bit glum. I put the party hat on wonky, I blew the party whistle dejectedly and I got it in one take. I put it in black and white and posted it online with no comment.

### ERIN

OMG. I sat up in bed and stopped scrolling on my phone.

Kiera is right! Kiera might actually be right about

something (again). God, no one tell her.

Grace has posted a sad photo on Instagram! Not just a slightly less fun one. A properly sad, black and white, poignant, arty photo. No captions. Not even that flattering.

She's sad! She misses me! Maybe? I mean I still shouldn't really overlook the fact that she's told me to get lost in no uncertain terms.

But maybe… This is my chance. This is my *in*. I could follow her to an airport now? (Maybe I really shouldn't be taking the advice of my eleven-year-old sister that seriously? Who watches too much Netflix … but she is nearly twelve.)

What exactly is my "airport moment"? And does Grace even *deserve* for me to try?

OK. OK. How about this: I try one airport moment. And if she doesn't go for it, I'll know it was never meant to be. I'll draw a line under it. Stop beating myself up and know there was nothing more I could have done. OK.

OK.

OK. Airport moment… Um…

I can't get her a *present*. I'm not rich like her.

There's nothing I have that she – oh wait there is

one thing that she wanted… *Hmmm*.

## *GRACE*

*Oh*. How strange – a text message from *Erin*!

"I'm very sorry. Would you like to come to my house (flat) for tea and I can explain? No worries if not, I will leave you alone. Srlsy."

Well.

Well, well, well.

I was unsure what to do.

I was very cross with Erin still. But I also missed her. But, also, I was very hurt by her betrayal. And then, of course, I was actually VERY curious to see her house.

Curiosity won out in the end.

# CHAPTER TWENTY-EIGHT

## Saturday 30ᵗʰ March

*ERIN*

I waited outside my building at 3pm for Grace to be dropped off.

I felt calm and nervous at the same time. Which was actually better than just plain old nervous, which is how I always used to feel.

I think I've made my peace with what I'm doing. If she bullies me mercilessly for how bad she thinks my flat is, then: (a) Kiera will have been wrong, so I can at least rub that in her face; (b) I'll know where I stand and stop trying; (c) I'll know that she actually isn't worth being friends with.

I like my flat. I'm (quite) happy there with my

mum and my sister. I'm not ashamed of it.

And really, what's the worst that can happen? I get *double* bullied? My life can't get doubly ruined. There is a double jeopardy indemnity clause about that. I'm pretty sure it applies to bullying too.

Grace's car pulled up and she stepped out. It's a busy road, so the car couldn't stay long and drove off with another car beeping at it.

"Hi Grace," I ventured. "Thanks for coming."

"Pleasure," said Grace dubiously, squinting up at my building.

"This way," I said, and she followed me inside.

We live in an old-fashioned block of flats with a tiny rickety elevator that only fits three people, with a sliding grate that you slide yourself and which I have enjoyed ever since we moved in.

"Is this safe?" Grace eyed the manual grate suspiciously.

"Oh yes," I smiled. "For up to three people. Think of it as having a shabby chic, kind-of-paired-down-but-still-sophisticated, Parisian vibe."

Grace's face lit up slightly at that. She maybe didn't *get* that I was vaguely satirising the differences between the tours of our houses.

"Yes, actually it is reminiscent of some..." she paused "...parts of Paris."

I think she was going to say "*run down* parts of Paris." (Where the murders happen.) But *still*, technically Paris.

We walked down the communal corridor to my flat. We could smell everyone's cooking. We reached my door and I undid all three locks, while Grace raised her eyebrows.

"So, this is my house," I said as we entered the narrow "hallway" that all rooms lead off. We had to squeeze up against each other so I could get the door shut behind us. It doesn't help that all our coats and shoes are in the way. (Mum keeps threatening to start running "a capsule household" but I don't think even she really knows what that means.)

"So, this is the living room and kitchen," I lead her one step to the left.

"Oh! Does it go on? No. Oh I see, yes. It's a kitchen-come-lounge. Lovely!" said Grace.

"Bathroom," I continued. We poked our heads in there.

"No way!" cried Grace. Then, "*cuuute*," in a vaguely apologetic way.

230

"That's Mum's room. And this is my bedroom. Mine and Kiera's."

We fully entered my bedroom. It was a tight squeeze.

"Hi, I'm Kiera," said my sister, standing up and proffering her hand, which Grace duly shook. "Would you like to sit on the chair?" Kiera waved at the tiny swivel stool that we usually kept stuffed under the plank (desk).

"Um. Where will you sit?" asked Grace.

"We can just sit on the lower bunk," said Kiera. "Guests get the fancy chair." She grinned to show she knew it wasn't *really* fancy, but Grace seemed unsure whether Kiera really thought this bent, squeaky thing was great. "I'm kidding, it's a wreck – come sit on our threadbare throne," added Kiera.

"Ha, alliteration," said Grace and I at the same time.

"Wow, you're both so different," remarked Kiera, dryly. I frowned at her. "Tea?" she offered.

"Thank you," said Grace benevolently. She sat down stiffly, and the chair squeaked.

"Brilliant, cheers," I said.

Kiera has been allowed to use the kettle by herself since she was ten and is still very proud of her tea-making skills.

"And biscuits?" she continued. "Me and Mum made some earlier. Not for *you*," she added hastily (and a bit rudely) to Grace. "Because she'd promised me we'd do baking."

"Sounds lovely," said Grace, politely.

Kiera left, and I sat down on the lower bunk.

"So," I said.

"So," echoed Grace.

I took a deep breath. "Look," I said, "I'm really sorry I told you the wrong deadline for the competition. I was very angry and upset that you threw me out of your party, and I wanted to get you back. I didn't expect you to apologise to me, and I should have come clean when you did. I can't get you a sorry present like you did for me, because I don't have any money, but you said you wanted to see my house, so here it is."

Graced stared at me, her expression unreadable. Then she reached out and clasped my arm, and said earnestly, "I'm really sorry too."

I wasn't sure what to say to that. Grace seemed

on the verge of some kind of emotion. "Um. That's cool. Um. Yay? Do we forgive each other then?"

"Yes!" Grace beamed. "And I'm sorry for what you would call bullying again in English."

"Because it is called bullying," I said.

"Yay, friends again!" Grace sidestepped this and gave my arm another squeeze.

"Yay!" I tried to join in the level of excitement but found it a bit awkward.

The moment passed. Grace let go of my arm and sat up a bit more stiffly. "Thank you for showing me your home. It's lovely. How did you know I wanted to see it so much?"

"Because you kept going on about it, and I get the feeling you don't like being told *no*."

Grace smiled, trying to compose herself, then theatrically clasped her hand in front of her heart. "I feel *seen*," she giggled, and I laughed.

"Your family seems nice," said Grace.

Just then the front door slammed.

We could hear someone muttering, "Idiots!" Then, "What have I told you about leaving shoes everywhere? This is a trip hazard. One of these days there'll be an injury!"

Then, "Ohhhh good timing! Yes please, tea for me!"

Grace looked at me quizzically.

"My mum's home," I said.

# CHAPTER TWENTY-NINE

**GRACE**

I had a surprisingly lovely time at Erin's house (flat). Abode. Let's go with that.

I think I've been on an emotional rollercoaster lately and it's difficult to get down in my diary my thoughts and feelings about what's been happening. (Even for *me* – a brilliant writer!) So that's some indication of how much of a rollercoaster it's been.

Anyway.

Erin has really stepped up as a friend and done her best to make it up to me after her deception. (Really it just comes down to character weakness and reluctance to tell the truth) but she is really sorry and has gone out of her way to show me so. And not

everyone can be as brilliant as me, and I fully admit that she was somewhat provoked.

Anyway.

I had a lovely time and met her and her mum and her sister and found them all very pleasant.

Weirdly, even though they are so different to *my* family, Erin's mother sort of reminded me of my dad. In that she's very forthright and *tells it like it is*. But kinder. I think I find much comfort in the consistency of people that tell it straight.

Once Erin's mother was home, everyone decided to have tea and biscuits (gingerbread men as it turned out – homemade). I was wracking my brains, but I don't think I've ever done any home baking. Maybe when I was very little with Mona? And obviously at school, but it's not quite the same.

We sat in the living room. So they all squeezed on to their sofa and let me sit on the only other chair in that room, in front of the fridge. (They have lovely guest etiquette, which I appreciated.)

And as I say, it was surprisingly lovely.

I was giving such long interesting answers to their questions that at one point, Erin's mother, Jo, said, "It's not an interview, love." And everyone laughed, but kindly.

At one point, Kiera told Jo about how she was disappointed with a mark she'd received on a maths test at school, and she said something along the lines of, "What's the point of even trying?"

And Jo responded, "It's not *failure*, it's *feedback* Kiera." (Which I *really* liked.) "Now you know what you have to do differently next time."

I was struck by what a brilliant and extraordinary family motto this was.

It was very similar in some ways to *my* family's motto, "*Second place is first loser,*" but a much more positive spin on the same idea. I really liked this reframe.

Then Erin and I went and hung out in her bedroom and chatted and stuff.

"So, what's happening with *the boy*?" I asked her.

"Nick? Oh, nothing."

"Nothing?"

"Beyond liking a couple of photos, no."

"That's a shame," I commented. "You seem a bit more confident these days; I thought maybe you would go for it."

"Well, I thought maybe something would happen

at your party…" Erin didn't need to finish that sentence.

"Well … stuff *did* happen at that party," I quipped. "I am so sorry by the way, again, for chucking you out. I'm not surprised you lied to me about the deadline, and I cringe every time I remember it."

"It is honestly fine," I replied. "I regret lying to you so much. I'm really sorry too."

"And I'm actually *glad* you hit Theo. He's *horrible*. Have you made up with Nicole?"

"No, she hates me."

"I don't think she does. I think she was just scared you'd leave her behind."

"How or why?" Erin asked me, a little incredulous. "She was always the cool one. I'm a nobody."

"You are *not* a nobody," I chastised her. "You're actually much more interesting than my initial impression of you."

"None taken," Erin grinned.

"And you've changed even since *I've* known you, so it must be weird for Nicole."

"What do you mean I've changed?"

"In a good way." I waved my hand vaguely. "You stuck up for yourself with us. Brave. You *used* to not

even make eye contact. Now you beat people up."
We both paused to laugh, then I continued. "And
maybe Nicole *liked* that you were so reliant on her. I
don't know. I don't really know the situation."

"I just don't fit anywhere," said Erin sadly. "I
didn't fit with *your* friends because I'm not cool,
and I said *on fleek*. I don't always fit brilliantly with
Nicole because I'm not cool, and don't know enough
about music. And, also, I said *on fleek* again. To tell
her I'd said it the first time," she explained.

"I mean, it sounds like you just need to stop saying
*on fleek*," I joked.

"Right?" Erin grinned. "Well, at least *you* get me."

"You know what though?" I said. "Why *should*
you have to keep trying to fit in with everyone? All
this time I've been giving you makeovers and stuff.
Why does no one meet you half way? And me. I
mean, granted, I have much more natural charisma,
but even I sometimes grow tired of the *cool game*."

"So, you want to form a new gang?" Erin suggested.
"An uncool one, where *we* make the rules?"

"Maybe." I paused.

"OK, I can get behind that," said Erin. "We'll form
a *new gang*, with all the best bits of both of ours.

We'll keep your confidence and wit," she gestured to me.

"Thank you," I smiled.

"And my ability to be genuine, and not bully people that are different."

"*Ouch*. But fair," I said. I paused in thought again. "God. Isn't it *so weird* that we're even friends?"

"*So* weird," agreed Erin instantly. "I really like you. But I sometimes don't fully understand why."

"I really like you too," I beamed. "But you know, ditto."

"OK," said Erin. "Well. Maybe it's time to tell Mrs Wilson that we think we're ready for her to broaden out the Charlotte Brontë Fan Club? Tell her we'd like to invite new members? We can make our writing group the civilisation we've always wanted to live in."

"Ooooh. Interesting!" I exclaimed. "I like this! Though... Don't want to be negative, just trouble-shooting here... No one seems to really *like* Charlotte Brontë apart from us. We may struggle to recruit new members."

"But isn't that the point? We'll be picky," said Erin.

"Also, again, don't mean to nitpick," I continued.

"We haven't really *covered* much Charlotte Brontë in the writing group. It's all kinds of other writing exercises. It's like a false advertising title."

"We are *fans* of hers, though. It's not totally false," protested Erin.

"We're fans of lots of stuff," I said.

"Are we? She's like the main thing we have in common," argued Erin.

"I can name *loads* of other things we're both fans of," I began, then sort of paused. "Um… Well… *Each other*."

We both laughed.

"The Weird Friends Fan Club," Erin grinned.

"I actually kind of like that," I said.

"Me too."

"And it will actually tell people what it is. A place where people you wouldn't expect to be friends can hang out with each other."

"And be fans of stuff. And do writing exercises," said Erin, grinning. "Also sounds a bit like the other members will be *our* fans."

"Yeah. It works. I'm not changing it," I grinned back.

"And *some* of our friends might want to join. But

they have to be nice to us, or they're out," said Erin.

"Yes, we'll have a code of conduct," I agreed. "I'm inviting Nick Brooker to join." I tried a cheeky wink.

"Did you just wink at me?"

I decided to brush over it. "And I'll invite Chloe. She could really benefit actually, get her grades up. I'm not saying she's stupid or anything. But she can't even feed her hamster properly. Have you seen how fat it is on Instagram?"

# CHAPTER THIRTY

**Sunday 31st March**

*ERIN*

I was totally waiting for Mum to *hate* Grace (like she hated Nic for having a mum that played tennis and being richer than us).

I mean, *come on*. Grace is a full-on landed gentry *snob* compared to Nicole. (In my mum's eyes – *I* like her now – obviously.)

After Grace left, I kept thinking, *here come the comments. Here we go* … but *nothing*. She didn't even remark on how Grace made water go everywhere when she used our tiny, hand-sized sink in the bathroom. (I *had* warned her about that, but everyone forgets the first time they use it.)

But anyway, eventually I had to go and *probe* Mum for it. "So, what did you think of *Grace*?" I stood in the doorway of the kitchen-lounge while Mum chopped carrots to make us a hearty soup.

"Hmm? Oh yes. *Lovely girl!* Bit intense."

"Bit intense?" I queried. "Is that a euphemism for…?"

"Being intense." Mum looked up at me briefly then went back to what she was doing.

"What, seriously? You actually think she's lovely? You don't hate her like you hate Nicole?"

"Oh, for the last time, Erin, I don't hate Nicole!" Mum replied tiredly. "I just don't know that she offers much … *challenge* for you." *Rude*.

"What about Nic's mum?" I pushed it.

Mum looked up at me mutely for a second, then changed the subject and said, "Grace seems like a lovely, funny, interesting, bright and vivacious person. She cares about good grades – which some other people could benefit from…" This was directed at Kiera as she lay on the sofa watching Netflix. "But she also seemed a bit intense and like she might be happier if she relaxed a bit and put less pressure on herself."

244

And that was that. My expectations were confounded.

And of course *Kiera* liked her too. Later, on Saturday night, when we were lying in bed, she commented about how interesting (if a tiny bit strange) Grace is, and even had the nerve to gloat about how right she'd been about everything.

What is it with my family suddenly seeing the inherent good in people all of a sudden?

### GRACE
And yet another brilliant poem by Grace Abella:

**Whatever the weather**
*The wind can howl*
*The rain can fall*
*The wolves can prowl*
*The songbirds call*

*And when they call*
*They call to me*
*And tell me the stories*
*Of how life can be*

*I watch the songbirds*
*Stick together*
*Flying together*
*Whatever the weather*

*And I know if I*
*Should cross the sea*
*We'll be safe together*
*Come wind, rain or thundery*

#naileditagain

I am so good at everything. #practisingselflove
And I am in *business mode*.

Today, at another wonderful lunch with Daddy, I announced, "Daddy. I think we need to have a little chat about the possible updating of our family motto."

Needless to say, #negotiatedthehelloutofthat #whataminotgoodat

And Daddy actually really likes "It's not failure, it's feedback", so that's a result.

And I have made the executive decision to re-gift the makeup present to Erin. It was her sorry

246

present after all, and I can't take back hers and we are friends again now.

#businessmode #unstoppable

### *ERIN*

I have this weird feeling in my stomach as I'm going to bed on Sunday night. It's like butterflies, but without the usual sense of dread that goes with it... I think I'm... I think I'm *looking forward* to school on Monday.

*Eurgh.* My weird transition to becoming Grace is complete. Haha, it's not that bad.

#notthatbad #iloveschoolnowbabes #apartfromnicoleisstillnotspeakingtome

# CHAPTER THIRTY-ONE

**Monday 1st April**

*GRACE*

OMG Chloe's hamster had babies! That's why it's got so fat! Actually very exciting. Those tiny babies looked sooo cute on Instagram.

#whatawonderfulworld #miracleoflifebabes

*ERIN*

There was an envelope on my desk when I arrived in the form room before registration. Nic was looking at me, but trying to pretend she wasn't.

I picked it up. "Is this from you?" I asked her. She nodded sheepishly.

"I have got you something, to say sorry. And

I would like us to be friends again," she said. I stared at her incredulous. Nic continued, "I'm not good at stuff like this – look, my hands are shaking." She held up a hand. "Open it!" She tried a smile.

"Is – are you… *Look, is this an April Fools' trick?*" I blurted out suspiciously.

"*What?!* No! God, of course not! Open it."

I picked up the envelope doubtfully.

"And I open it, and it's anthrax and then you go *'PSYCH!'* and laugh at me," I added.

Nic chuckled, "Well I wouldn't say *psych* because –" she caught herself before insulting me, "I would say 'April Fools', but I'm not going to. Please open it."

I opened it. It was cute card that said "Sorry" on it, and inside was a ticket to see *The Crumples*. Nic had written:

Dear Erin,
I'm really sorry that I didn't handle you leaving me in English better. I shouldn't have teased you. I will try not to call you swot any more (sometimes they just slip out, winky face).

I hope we can be best friends again.
Lots of love,
Nic XXX


PS — WANNA SEE THE CRUMPLES WITH ME?! O
MAH GAAAAWWWWD!!!!!!!!!

I smiled, then frowned. "Are you *sure* this isn't a trick?"

"*Yes!* Oh my god, woman! I'm so bad at saying sorry, don't drag it out!" She stood up and hugged me. I hugged her back. "I love you, you doofus." We pulled apart and she looked at me. "You don't have to say it back, whatever."

I laughed, genuinely. "You know I do," I said. "I sometimes find it hard to say when—"

"I know. I'll get better at listening. And stop interrupting. I get it. I get what I just did there."

"Cool," I beamed.

"Aw, I think I might cry." Liz had been watching us and looked moved.

"Ha, hashtag better than EastEnders," I joked.

"Well, let's not go nuts," said Liz, recovering from her emotion.

Grace came over then. "Oh, did you guys make up?"

I nodded.

"That's great. You ready?"

"Yes." Then another thought occurred to me. "Oh hey, now we're friends again, Nic, Liz, do you want to join our new writing group?"

"Is this an April Fools?" said Nic.

## GRACE

"Guys, everyone, can I have your attention please?"

My girl squad looked up to see me standing at their desks, flanked by Erin, Nicole and Liz.

"Uh-oh," said Brianna.

"Oh god, *now what*?" said Sylvie.

"Cute hamster babies," Liz told Chloe.

"Thanks!"

"Guys, listen." I thought I'd better take charge of the situation. "This is Erin and she is my friend."

"*Urgghhh*." Sylvie rolled her eyes and groaned. "Not *again*. We've been here before. She *lied* to you, remember?"

"Talk about *déjà vu*," agreed Brianna.

"Yes," I agreed. "But now we are friends again.

And I want all my friends to get along. And this is Nicole and Liz, and they're fine too."

"Nope, nope, nope," said Sylvie.

"Is this an April Fools?" demanded Brianna.

"Oh my god, *is it*?" Sylvie seized on this. "It's actually very good if so."

"No," I said.

"It so is! We're not falling for it!" Brianna grinned.

"They'd have to be *friends* to agree to go along with that," Chloe pointed out perceptively.

"*Urgghhh*," said Sylvie. "It's really not a trick?"

I shook my head.

"Really, *really*?"

"No."

We *maybe* could have picked a better day to do all this.

"You love her, you hate her. I mean, *my god*, just *pick* something already," snapped Brianna.

"I *have*." I said this with as much gravitas as possible (which is a lot, because this is me we're talking about) so they'd know I was serious.

"All right, fine, *whatever*." Sylvie looked bored and swung back on her chair slightly.

"And *furthermore*," I continued grandly, "I can now

announce, that *our exclusive* new writers group, the Weird Friends Fan Club, is accepting new members. So, if any of you would like to join, you would be welcome. We meet on Monday lunchtimes."

#nailedit #whataminotgoodatbabes

━━━▶

EMAIL
16.42
FROM: MRS WILSON
TO: WEIRD FRIENDS FAN CLUB
SUBJECT: IT'S OFFICIAL!!

Dear Grace and Erin,
Further to our conversation at lunchtime, I'm delighted you're bringing new, passionate writers into the group! And I'm delighted we could find a day to settle on that didn't clash with netball.

The Sixth Form common room (corner) is now booked for your use every Monday for the first half of lunch. I won't always be able to make it, but will pop in when I can, and am always on hand via email for advice etc.

A couple of tips for you both:

#

– I suggest you take it in turns to chair the meetings. You both know what to do now.

– Focus on keeping order; sometimes with bigger groups the subject gets away and it can be hard to keep the discussion on track.

Have fun!

I'm SO pleased this project is off to such a fantastic start.

Good luck!

Best,

**Mrs Wilson**

*Second in Department for English*

# CHAPTER THIRTY-TWO

**Monday 8th April**

*ERIN*

"It gives me great pleasure to call to order the first official meeting of the all new Weird Friends Fan Club!" I announced to clapping.

"Shouldn't I have said that?" asked Grace. "No? OK. I mean, you did a great job too." (I looked at her.) "Really? Is this another example of me doing *that thing*? Well, OK."

"Anyway," I continued, addressing the group of Nic, Liz, Chloe, Sylvie, Brianna, Si Adoki and Nick Brooker. "Today we are going to discuss how we do this writing group: you can ask any questions, and then we will set ourselves a short story writing

exercise that we can all discuss next week."

"It's all about the planning, isn't it?" said Liz. "That's what I heard."

"Well, some writers work that way," I replied.

"No, no, *don't* plan," said Nic. "You can plan too much. Don't fence yourself in. It's like that saying, '*If you want to make God laugh, tell him your plans'*."

"That's crazy," responded Chloe. "God can watch any YouTube prank videos he wants. He doesn't need my plans." Si Adoki and Brianna laughed.

"OK. Let's get back on track," I said. Everyone looked at me. Nick Brooker even smiled. I smiled back and also kind of squinted. Damn.

"Do you think they have YouTube in heaven though?" asked Chloe.

"Oh my god, your hamster babies are so cute…"

Honestly, diary – I'm not even exaggerating. That's what everyone wanted to talk about.

"*People*, there are writing competitions that we need to enter and prepare for," chided Grace.

"Can I write about my hamster?"

"Is everyone going to write about hamsters?"

Although, to be fair, this is almost exactly how

I always imagined a Year Nine literary discussion would go: veering off on to loads of tangents…

But what a fun lunchtime.

# ACKNOWLEDGEMENTS

Massive thanks to Kirsty Stansfield, Suzy Jenvey, Lindsey Fraser, Kathryn Ross, Kate Wilson, Catherine Stokes, Fiona Scoble, Nicola Theobald, Tom Bonnick, Rebecca Mason, Julia Kathro, Lauren Fairgrieve, Karen O'Leary and everyone at Nosy Crow, who have been so fantastic. And also thank YOU for reading.